Gertie's Leap to Greatness

Gertie's Leap to Greatness

Kate Beasley

Illustrations by
Jillian Tamaki

FARRAR STRAUS GIROUX / *New York*

Farrar Straus Giroux Books for Young Readers
175 Fifth Avenue, New York 10010

Printed in the United States of America by
R. R. Donnelley & Sons Company, Harrisonburg, Virginia
First edition, 2016
1 3 5 7 9 10 8 6 4 2
mackids.com

Library of Congress Cataloging-in-Publication Data

Names: Beasley, Kate, author. | Tamaki, Jillian, 1980– illustrator.
Title: Gertie's leap to greatness / Kate Beasley ; with illustrations by Jillian Tamaki.
Description: First edition. | New York : Farrar, Straus and Giroux, 2016. |
   Summary: "Gertie is a girl on a mission to be the best fifth grader ever in order
   to show her estranged mother that Gertie doesn't need her—not one bit!"—
   Provided by publisher.
Identifiers: LCCN 2015030871 | ISBN 9780374302610 (hardback) |
   ISBN 9780374302627 (e-book)
Subjects: | CYAC: Abandoned children—Fiction. | Mothers—Fiction. | Schools—
   Fiction. | BISAC: JUVENILE FICTION / Family / General (see also headings
   under Social Issues). | JUVENILE FICTION / Humorous Stories.
Classification: LCC PZ7.1.B433 Ge 2016 | DDC [Fic]—dc23
LC record available at http://lccn.loc.gov/2015030871

Our books may be purchased in bulk for promotional, educational, or business
use. Please contact your local bookseller or the Macmillan Corporate and
Premium Sales Department at (800) 221-7945 ext. 5442 or by e-mail at
MacmillanSpecialMarkets@macmillan.com.

Contents

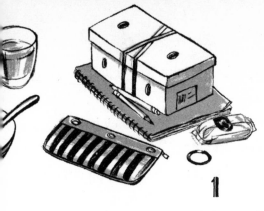

1

A Monstrosity of Science

THE BULLFROG WAS ONLY HALF DEAD, WHICH WAS PERFECT.

He hunkered in the dark culvert under the driveway and gazed at Gertie Reece Foy with a tragical gleam in his eye, as if he knew that her face was the last lovely thing he would ever see.

Gertie stuck her head and shoulders in the culvert and grabbed the frog. His fat legs dangled over her fingers.

She ran to the house and pushed the kitchen door open with her back. Laying the frog on the counter, she ripped open the drawer that held all the unusual and exciting kitchen equipment. She rummaged through cheese graters, bottle openers, and tongs, glancing up every other second to make sure the frog hadn't moved or, worse, *died*.

"What's going on in there?" Aunt Rae yelled from the living room.

"Nothing!" Gertie whipped out the turkey baster.

She wiggled her index finger between the frog's lips—if you could call them lips—and poked the pipette into his mouth. Then she squeezed the blue bulb at the other end, forcing oxygen into his lungs.

The air must have revived him quickly, or maybe he was a little less dead than Gertie had hoped, because he sprang for the edge of the counter. Gertie lunged sideways and cupped her hands over him.

"There, there," she said. "You're safe now."

She peeked at him through her fingers, and he peeked back at her, his eyeballs quivering with gratitude. Or maybe they quivered with rage. It was hard to tell.

She wrapped her hands around the frog's middle, turned on her heel, and crashed into a soft, flowery stomach.

"Oof," said Aunt Rae. She blinked at the frog in Gertie's hands. "What in the Sam Hill are you doing?"

"I resuscitated him." Gertie held the frog closer.

Aunt Rae moved to stand over the air vent in the kitchen floor, and her housedress ballooned around her legs. "You what?"

"Resuscitated," said Gertie. "It means I brought him back to life."

"I *know* what it means." Aunt Rae swayed her weight from foot to foot. *"Why'd* you resuscitate a ugly old bullfrog? That's what I don't know."

Gertie sighed. She spent a lot of time explaining things that should have been obvious to people. "I did it so he could become a miracle of science," she said.

"Huh." Aunt Rae wrinkled her nose at the frog. "Looks more like a monstrosity of science to me."

Gertie gasped. "Oh my Lord."

"What?"

"Aunt Rae, that's even better!"

The monstrosity of science wriggled in her hands, and Gertie tried to hold him tighter but not so much tighter that his eyes would pop right out of his head and fall on the floor.

"I've got to get him in his box, Aunt Rae," Gertie said, "before his eyes roll around on the floor and we have to stick them back."

"Why would—" Aunt Rae began.

"Oh my Lord! I don't have time to explain every little detail!"

"All right, all right." Aunt Rae patted down her skirt.

"But I want you to use bleach on my counter when you're done, you hear me?"

Gertie put the frog and some nice wet leaves in a shoe box. Then she rubber-banded on the lid and went out to the porch. The Zapper-2000, a bug zapper big enough to fry baby dragons, hung from the rafters.

Phase One of the mission was off to a good start.

Gertie always had at least one mission in the works, and she never, *ever* failed to complete her missions. It didn't matter that she wasn't the fastest or the smartest or the tallest, because what made Gertie a force to be reckoned with was the fact that she never gave up. Not ever. Her father liked to say that she was a bulldog with its jaws locked on a car tire.

Gertie was thinking about having that printed on business cards she could hand out to people.

She crouched in the fluorescent blue beam of light beneath the Zapper-2000 and collected a handful of the mosquito bodies that littered the ground. As she worked, the cicadas and crickets started sawing their night song. Gertie stood and watched the sun set on the last day of summer vacation.

With these tasty mosquitoes, the bullfrog was sure to be fat and croaky tomorrow. And with a fat and croaky bullfrog to take with her, Gertie was sure to have the best summer speech of any student at Carroll Elementary. She curled her toes over the edge of the porch boards.

She, Gertie Reece Foy, was going to be the greatest fifth grader in the whole school, world, and universe!

And that was just Phase One.

2
You're in My Seat

GERTIE HAD A REASON FOR WANTING TO BE THE GREATEST fifth grader in the world. Two days before the resuscitation of the bullfrog, something big had happened. She had seen a sign.

Not the kind of Sign with a capital *S* that people saw in crystal balls or tea leaves or unusual mold formations on cheese. No. Gertie had seen a Sunshine Realty sign.

The sign was in front of the house where Gertie's mother lived, and it said *For Sale by Sunshine Realty.* That sign was the reason Gertie was on her most important mission yet. And it was the reason why, when she woke up on the first morning of fifth grade, she launched herself out of bed, ran to the bathroom, and brushed her teeth with extra froth in front of the mirror.

Gertie had brown hair which she wore in a ponytail that stuck straight out the top of her head, which encouraged blood flow to her brain, which made her have lots of ideas. She also had a biggish nose and a pointy chin. She had freckles on her face, and she had elbows halfway down her arms. As always, she looked exactly like herself.

She pointed her toothbrush at her reflection. "This is your moment," she said, and she wiped away her toothpaste beard.

In her bedroom, she put on shorts, her favorite blue T-shirt, and the twenty-five-percent-off sandals Aunt Rae had bought her. Then she fastened a gold locket around her neck. Gertie dropped the locket down the front of her shirt and picked up the shoe box, enjoying the weight it had to it. Nothing, she decided, was as comforting as the weight of a nice, healthy bullfrog.

When Gertie marched into the kitchen, Aunt Rae held out a package of Twinkies, and Gertie snatched it out of the air with her free hand. She stepped through the screen door, then stopped and tilted her head, waiting.

"Give 'em hell, baby," called Aunt Rae.

Gertie tapped the Twinkies to her brow in a salute and let the door bang shut behind her.

On the bus, Gertie sat next to one of her two best friends. His name was Junior Parks.

Junior had a lot of nervous energy, which must have burned up a lot of calories, because he was the skinniest boy in their class. He was so skinny that some people said he had worms, which he didn't, but Gertie would've been friends with him even if he did, because she wasn't squeamish about worms.

Junior was probably so nervous because of his name. His name wasn't Mitchell Parks Jr. or Benji Parks Jr. His father's name was Junior Parks. So Junior's name was Junior Parks *Jr.*

He always introduced himself as Junior Parks the Second, but everyone still called him Junior Jr.

"What's in the box?" Junior asked the moment Gertie sat down.

You could always count on Junior to notice little details. He was worried that anything new might be a threat to him. For instance, right now he was probably afraid that the box held something horrible, like a severed hand or a dead rat or a nice present for everyone in the class except him.

Gertie settled the shoe box in her lap and patted the lid. "You'll have to wait and see, won't you?" She nibbled a Twinkie. Most people thought the middles were plain cream-filled, but she could taste a hint of lemon.

Junior gnawed his lip.

Gertie gave in. A little. "It's for my summer speech."

Junior's eyes widened, and his shoes kicked the seat in front of him. "I forgot about the summer speech," he said in a strangled voice.

"*How* could you forget something this important?" Gertie asked.

On the first day of school, every class at Carroll Elementary spent the morning on the summer speeches. Each student stood in front of their class and told the one most interesting thing that had happened that summer. The teachers said the speeches weren't a competition, but the students knew better.

In first grade, Gertie hadn't known about the speeches, so she hadn't been prepared. She'd only stumbled through, trying at the last moment to think of something juicy.

In second grade, she had carefully reviewed her summer

and chosen what *had* to be the most interesting event—when she'd eaten fifteen oysters without throwing up. But that was the year Roy Caldwell had climbed up a pecan tree and refused to come down for two whole days, just so he would have the best story.

In third grade, Gertie *should* have won with her reenactment of what had happened on the oil rig where her father worked. Now, that had been a humdinger of a summer speech.

The important thing wasn't what you told, but how you told it. It was one thing to say that your father was working on an oil rig. It was another thing altogether if you said that alarms had gone off because one of the pumps was under pressure, and everybody had jumped off the platform and into the shark-and-eel-infested ocean.

Unfortunately, that was the same summer Ella Jenkins had had her appendix taken out in the hospital, and she had a lumpy purple scar to prove it.

Gertie didn't even want to *think* about the fourth-grade speeches when Leo Riggs had shaved off his left eyebrow.

But this year was Gertie's year. It had to be. She licked the last of the greasy yellow Twinkie crumbs off her fingers as the bus turned onto Jones Street. Gertie scooted to the edge of her seat.

The houses on Jones Street seemed impressively housey to Gertie. Aunt Rae's house had flaky paint and crooked doorframes. These houses had straight rows of brick and graceful columns and brass knockers that gleamed on tall front doors.

But that wasn't the most interesting thing about Jones Street.

The most interesting thing was that Gertie's mother lived there. Her name was Rachel Collins.

When Gertie was just a baby, Rachel had gone off to live in the house on Jones Street. The only things she'd left behind were the locket, Gertie's father, and Gertie.

Gertie's father, Frank Foy, said that Rachel Collins had left because she wasn't happy and she had to leave to find out if something else would make her happy.

Gertie thought that wasn't any kind of reason to leave. After all, sometimes she wasn't happy about going to school, but she had to anyway. And she was never happy about going to church, but Aunt Rae dragged her along. And plenty of times she was very not happy with Aunt Rae when she wouldn't let Gertie stay up late or wear her pajamas to the grocery store. But she never *left* Aunt Rae.

Gertie's father explained that Rachel Collins had been a different kind of unhappy. For her, being with them was like wearing a pair of shoes that were too tight. You could limp along for a while, but your feet would just hurt more and more until you were sure that if you walked one step further in those shoes, they'd squeeze your toes off.

Gertie said that plenty of people did just fine without toes.

But it didn't matter what Gertie thought, because Rachel had stepped out of Frank and Gertie's life and into the housiest house on Jones Street, where a big poplar tree grew in the front yard and where now a Sunshine Realty sign was stuck in trimmed grass.

The sign still said *For Sale.*

Gertie sighed and leaned back against the bus seat.

Rachel Collins's house was for sale because she was moving away because she was getting married to a man named Walter who lived in Mobile with his own family. Everyone around town was talking about it.

Most kids would probably be upset if their mother was getting married to a strange man named Walter and leaving forever and didn't even tell them about it, but Gertie was not most kids.

She was absolutely not upset, because she had a plan. More than a plan. She had a mission.

Now she touched the front of her shirt so that the

locket could remind her of what she had to do. As soon as she gave the best summer speech and claimed her rightful position as the greatest fifth grader in the world, she would launch Phase Two. She was going to take the locket back to her mother. She'd show up on her mother's front porch, gleaming with greatness, swinging the locket on its chain, and she'd say, breezy as a gale-force wind, *Didn't want you to forget this while you were packing.* And then Rachel Collins would know that Gertie Foy was one-hundred-percent, not-from-concentrate awesome and that she didn't need a mother anyway. So there.

Gertie patted the shoe box.

"It's a bullfrog," she told Junior in a voice low enough that the other kids wouldn't hear.

"Wow." Junior looked even more miserable. "Bet your speech is going to be good."

Junior never did well at speeches. He got so nervous that his feet started kicking around, and he wound up knocking over desks and bruising people's shins. But Gertie was an excellent public speaker because she practiced all the time in front of the bathroom mirror.

"It'll be the best," she promised.

* * *

As they walked to their new classroom, Gertie was careful not to let her fingers cover the air holes on the shoe box.

She pushed through the noisy students and set her shoe box on a desk in the front row. Junior put his bag on the chair beside hers, his arms swinging by his sides even though he wasn't walking anymore.

Gertie's classmates were choosing seats, saying hello to friends they hadn't seen all summer, and arranging new school supplies in their cubbies. Jean Zeller was turning away from the pencil sharpener.

Jean was Gertie's other best friend, and she was the smartest person Gertie had ever met. A long time ago, Roy Caldwell and his friends had called her Jean-ius to tease her, but Jean had liked the nickname so much that she had started writing it at the top of her assignments. Jean blew the shavings off her lethally sharp pencil points and walked over to Gertie and Junior.

"They're number twos," Jean said, brandishing the pencils. "I made sure they were number twos. What kind are yours?" She narrowed her eyes at Junior's empty desk.

"Umm." Junior unzipped his bag and peered inside. "Yellows?"

Jean rolled her eyes. "It's okay, I brought extras."

Jean took the last seat in the front row, right beside Gertie. Gertie was sandwiched between her two best friends, holding a new pencil, and thinking that she'd accomplish this mission in record time, when something poked the back of her neck.

"You're in my seat."

3
Squish

The finger that had poked Gertie's neck was bony and had a pink-polished nail. Its owner was a yellow-haired girl who had green eyes and shimmery lip gloss.

"Did you hear me?" the girl said, and raised her eyebrows. "You're in my seat."

Gertie reassured herself that *her* shoe box with *her* frog was sitting on top of *her* desk before she answered the girl. "I'm already sitting here," she said.

"Yes, but I'm *new* here." The girl crossed her arms and began to tap her foot, waiting for Gertie to move out of her way.

Kids who had been examining each other's new shoes and haircuts looked up at the girl.

"Well, we're *old* here," Jean said, and crossed her arms, too.

The foot stopped tapping.

"But we could move," said Junior quickly, looking from one girl to another. "We could sit in the back or just go away somewhere and . . . and . . ."

Gertie stared at Junior until his voice dried up like a raisin.

"But Ms. Simms *said* I could sit here." The girl smiled. "Because I'm new. I need to sit in the front so I can keep up with everything."

New people weren't the only ones who had special reasons for needing to sit in the front. For instance, Gertie needed the front because when they watched movies she didn't want to have to look past other people's heads. And Jean liked the front row because she needed to make sure teachers saw her when she raised her hand. And Junior Jr. *hated* the front row, but he had to sit there anyway to be with Gertie and Jean.

"Ms. Simms didn't say any such thing," Gertie said.

"Yes, I did."

The new girl smiled at someone standing behind Gertie. Slowly, Gertie turned around to see a woman wearing red high heels. Gertie tilted her head way back to face her new teacher. Ms. Simms had square shoulders, round glasses, and a dimple in her chin. She was looking right into Gertie's face, and she was smiling. Not the stretchy smile that some adults used for kids. She smiled like they were friends.

"Mary Sue wanted to be sure she didn't get left out of anything. She's new this year." Ms. Simms put a hand on Gertie's shoulder. "I told her she could sit here. All the other front-row seats are full. You don't mind moving, do you?"

Gertie minded.

But she wanted her new teacher to know that she was nice and agreeable, because she was. It was this new girl who *wasn't* being agreeable. She slowly started to move her shoe box.

"Thank you for understanding." Ms. Simms beamed at her.

"Oh, yes, thank you," said the new girl. She was one of those people who acted nicer when the teacher was watching.

"If Gertie moves," said Jean, "then we move, too." She snatched up her number twos.

Junior jumped up, knocking over his chair.

Gertie lifted her chin as she passed the new girl. *She* might have a front-row seat, but Gertie had two best friends, which was seventeen million times better.

The new girl settled herself into Gertie's desk and dusted the top with her sleeve. Gertie glared at the back of her head.

This new girl was a seat-stealer.

Once Gertie had figured out what this girl was and put a name to it, she felt better about the whole thing. *Seat-stealer,* she thought in the nastiest voice she could imagine, and she felt even better.

"I'm Ms. Simms." Gertie's new teacher wrote her name on the whiteboard and capped the marker with a *pop.* "And I can't wait to hear about all the adventures you had this summer." Ms. Simms looked at the attendance sheet. "Roy Caldwell, will you start for us?"

Roy's left arm was in a plaster cast that might have been lime green once but was now so covered in marker drawings that it was hard to tell. He'd probably broken the arm on purpose, just so he'd have the best summer speech.

When he got to the front of the room he pointed at his cast. "Bet you're wondering how I got this. I saw a show on one of those educational channels. I wasn't watching it for me," he said, "because I don't like educational stuff. That stuff's for losers."

Jean hissed.

"No interrupting," Ms. Simms said. "Be considerate."

Roy ran his good hand through his hair and grinned at Jean. "So anyway, it was about what happens to balloons when they float up to the atmosphere. How they blow apart into a million pieces, right? So I decided to try it on people. And I got a bunch of those Fourth of July balloons from the Piggly Wiggly and tied the strings to my belt loops—"

"What did your mother say about this?" Ms. Simms asked. It wasn't interrupting when the teacher was the one doing it.

"She likes it when I'm not in the house. Says I need the fresh air. Anyway, so I got more and more balloons until I started to feel kind of light . . ."

But Gertie didn't want to hear any more. Roy's speech was good. Maybe too good. She was holding her shoe box to her chest and rocking it gently, when Ewan Buckley dared to interrupt.

"My mom told me you broke your arm falling down the stairs," Ewan said.

"No inter—" began Ms. Simms.

"You hush your mouth!" said Roy at the same time.

The class gasped.

"Roy!" Ms. Simms leaped to her red high heels.

"I'm sorry! I wasn't talking to you, Ms. Simms." Roy's face actually turned white—something Gertie had only read about in books. "I meant Ewan! I—"

"Roy, sit down. Sit down right now."

"I would never tell you to hush *your* mouth," Roy said.

Gertie let out a breath she hadn't known she was holding. Roy was out of the running for best summer speech.

"Gertrude Foy," Ms. Simms called out.

Several people sniggered.

"It's Gertie." She stood up, walked to the front of the room, and faced the class. "In this box," she said without preamble, "is a frog."

The class stopped sniggering.

Gertie set the box on the seat-stealer's desk, and the new girl leaned back and cringed, like she was scared the frog would jump out and bite her head off.

"This frog was completely and utterly dead," Gertie told the class. "And in the name of science, I rushed him to my aunt Rae's kitchen. And using only everyday kitchen tools, I brought him back to life. That makes him"—she tore off the shoe box lid, grabbed the frog under his armpits, and raised him over her head—"a zombie frog."

The frog was lifted high, and everyone turned their faces up to see him—his long legs scrabbling against Gertie's arms, his green-brown skin gleaming in the sunlight that streamed through the window.

"Gosh he's big," Ewan said, and Ms. Simms was so stunned by the mega awesomeness of Zombie Frog that she forgot to tell Ewan not to interrupt.

"One day," said Gertie, "when I have a real laboratory, I'll be bringing people back to life just like I was Dr. Frankenstein."

"He was exactly *how* dead?" asked Ewan.

It was all in the telling. "*Utterly* dead. As a doornail."

Roy crossed his arms. "*How'd* you bring him back?"

"Turkey baster."

Roy frowned at the ceiling, thinking. Then he nodded.

"Can we see him?" asked Leo.

Gertie carried the frog around so that everyone could look straight into his resurrected eyeballs. When her classmates had appreciated him, she put Zombie Frog back in his box and snapped the rubber band around it.

"Thank you, Gertie," said Ms. Simms, and she wasn't giving anything away, but Gertie knew she had to be pleased.

Phase One was going to be an instant success.

After Gertie, Ella Jenkins talked about going to her

grandmother's house, which wasn't nearly as good as a zombie frog.

And Junior's speech was painful to watch. "Ummm," he said. "Well." He chewed on his thumbnail and stared at his shoes for so long that the class started laughing again, which made his shoulders hunch.

"Did you go on vacation?" Ms. Simms asked.

Junior looked up. "Like the beach or wilderness camping?"

"Exactly!" Ms. Simms smiled.

"No," said Junior, shaking his head. "No, I didn't do anything like that."

Roy blew a raspberry against the back of his hand, and Junior's neck turned pink.

"I spent the summer at my mom's salon," he said. He looked at Ms. Simms and pressed his lips together so tightly it was clear she'd need a crowbar to get another word out of him.

"Right. Thank you for sharing." Ms. Simms checked her list. "Mary Sue Spivey, will you take over from Junior?"

The seat-stealer stood and turned to face the class.

"I'm Mary Sue," she said. "I didn't know we were going to have to say anything. We don't do this at my school in California."

"You're from California?" asked Leo.

"Los Angeles," said Mary Sue. "My father's a film director. We only moved here because he's shooting a new Jessica Walsh movie nearby."

"Hold the mayo," said Roy. He banged his cast against his desk. "You know *Jessica Walsh*?"

Everyone stared, breathless, at Mary Sue. Jessica Walsh had her own television show and her own collection of sticker earrings and her own cotton-candy-scented shampoo.

Mary Sue looked at them all, sitting on the edges of their seats. "Of course," she said, lifting one shoulder. "My father is Martin Lorimer Spivey. He's directed lots of Jessica Walsh's films. He's filming in Alabama, so he brought me along." She pulled a phone from her pocket and started thumbing the buttons. "I think I have a picture with her."

Ms. Simms didn't mention that phones were against the rules. Instead, she went to look over Mary Sue's shoulder. "Oh my goodness, it's really her," she said.

Mary Sue passed around her phone.

Gertie looked at the picture of Mary Sue Spivey standing beside the most famous twelve-year-old movie star in the country before she handed the phone to Jean.

"I'm sure you'll have a lot of stories to share with us," said Ms. Simms. "We'll have to talk more later."

Mary Sue's speech had been interesting, but it wasn't because *she* was that interesting, thought Gertie. It was because Jessica Walsh was. But everyone was whispering and craning their necks to get a better look at the new girl, like *she* was the famous one.

"Thank you, everyone," said Ms. Simms when they'd finished. "I feel like I know all of you a little better. Mary Sue, you're new here, so you should know that we keep phones off and put away during class, please."

Gertie's heart lifted.

"And, Gertie," Ms. Simms said, "I think it would be best to release that impressive frog during recess, don't you?"

"What?" Gertie grabbed the corners of the box. "Can't I take him home and put him back in his culvert?"

"I'm sure he'll be just as happy here." Ms. Simms frowned at Roy as she said, "I'm sure he needs plenty of fresh air."

At recess, Gertie, Junior, and Jean carried Zombie Frog toward the back of the playground.

"What if he can't find his way back home?" Gertie said. "Do you know how horrible that would be? Lost. Cars almost running over you. *Squish*."

Junior shuddered.

Gertie trudged on, stopping where the trees grew right up against the sagging fence that marked the edge of the school property. She knelt and set the frog on the ground.

"He *is* an impressive frog." Junior scuffed his shoe against the leaves. "That's what Ms. Simms said. *Impressive.*"

Gertie hoped Ms. Simms had meant it. But if Ms. Simms had loved Zombie Frog, she wouldn't have wanted Gertie to get rid of him, would she? She would have wanted him to become their class mascot or pet or something. Gertie had thought Phase One was in the bag, but now she wasn't sure. Had Mary Sue's speech been better? Gertie had to be absolutely certain that she was the *very* best before she carried out Phase Two.

"It's ridiculous." Jean leaned against the fence. "Everyone likes her just because she's new." She didn't say which *her* she was talking about. "And rich. And kind of famous."

Zombie Frog eyed Junior's twitchy foot until Gertie nudged him, and when he hopped into the woods, he *did* hop with impressive leaps. Gertie watched him until he disappeared. She hoped he was impressive enough to hop himself far away to a better place.

On the other side of the playground, a small crowd had gathered around the new girl with yellow hair. It was possible, thought Gertie, that Mary Sue Spivey was something even worse than a seat-stealer.

4
What's a Mary Sue Spivey?

WHEN GERTIE GOT HOME, SHE SLAMMED THE SCREEN DOOR so that Aunt Rae would know she was back and would come and greet her. She waited. All alone. In the empty kitchen. She drooped her shoulders and hung her head so that her ponytail flopped over her face, and she was sure that she must have been the saddest little sight anybody ever saw.

Only nobody did see it, because nobody came to greet her.

Normally, somebody—her father when he was home or Aunt Rae or *somebody*—came to the door to tell her to wash the playground out from under her fingernails or to ask her what important things she'd done at school.

But today, when she was about to have a nervous breakdown because an evil seat-stealer was trying to ruin her entire life, nobody cared.

If Aunt Rae had really loved her, she would have been able to sense that Gertie was unhappy, like how dogs could smell fear and earthquakes and alien invasions, and she would've run to the kitchen, hollering, "Gertie, baby, what's *wrong*?"

Gertie added Aunt Rae's unlovingness to the long list of everything that had gone wrong that day. She sighed and dragged her bag through the kitchen.

When Gertie stepped into the living room, Audrey Williams was upside down on the sofa. Her feet stuck up over the back, and her head hung down over the edge of the seat cushions.

Aunt Rae and Gertie kept Audrey during the hours between when kindergarten ended and her parents finished work. Audrey was obsessed with a television program called *The Waltons*, which was about this big family that wore old-fashioned clothes and talked about how much they loved each other. Gertie thought it was the most boring show in the world.

"You're not supposed to watch TV," Gertie said, because it was true that Audrey wasn't supposed to watch television. Also, being responsible and bossy made Gertie feel grown-up.

Audrey's eyes reflected the images on the screen. She didn't make a move to turn the television off.

Sighing, Gertie reached for the remote, but Audrey snatched it away and rolled off the sofa. Gertie grabbed for her, and she dodged. Gertie lunged, and Audrey dived. She hopped on the coffee table and flittered back to the sofa.

When Audrey was once again watching television upside down with the remote resting on her stomach, Gertie asked, panting, "Where's Aunt Rae?"

Audrey pointed one foot toward the laundry room, and Gertie stomped over to the door.

"Oh my Lord! How can you be doing laundry at a time like this?"

Aunt Rae looked up from the shirt she was ironing. "Hey, Gertie, I didn't hear you come in."

"I don't know how you didn't," said Gertie. "I slammed the door as hard as I could."

"Really? Maybe I should check my hearing aid." She acted like she wasn't upset at all about Gertie's feelings or her own unlovingness.

She handed Gertie the shirt, hot off the ironing board. Gertie sighed and folded the shirt in half.

Aunt Rae swayed back and forth with the movement of the iron.

Gertie folded the shirt in half again and then again. She sighed one more time.

Aunt Rae kept ironing.

"Don't you hear me sighing?"

Aunt Rae looked surprised. "I thought you were just breathing extra loud today. Did something happen at school?"

Gertie gave up folding the shirt in halves and rolled it into a tidy log. "We did the summer speeches."

"What'd they think of your frog?" Aunt Rae asked. "Bet they never saw a resurrected frog before, huh?"

"Someone else did better," Gertie said.

"How'd they do better?" Aunt Rae yanked the iron cord out of the wall.

"It was just more . . . impressive," Gertie said. "I've got to be the most impressive person in my class."

"I already think you're very impressive." Aunt Rae took the shirt out of Gertie's hands, refolded it, and stacked all the laundry in a basket.

Gertie tried to let Aunt Rae's words make her feel better. But it wasn't enough for *Aunt Rae* to think she was impressive. She needed to prove it to Rachel Collins, too. "What can I do to be a better person?"

"You could play with Audrey. She's got a bad case of the mopes lately."

Gertie groaned. "Aunt Rae, I can't play with Audrey. She needs to play with her own kind." She had explained over and over to Aunt Rae that the only thing five-year-olds and ten-year-olds had in common was that they both had eyebrows. "Besides, I need to be more . . . more . . . more like . . ." Gertie threw her arms out and wiggled her fingers, trying to make Aunt Rae understand.

Aunt Rae stared at her.

"I need to be better than Mary Sue Spivey," Gertie blurted.

"What's a Mary Sue Spivey?"

"A no-good, seat-stealing new girl," Gertie answered at once.

"I bet she's not all that bad." Aunt Rae was determined to be unhelpful today.

"Jean doesn't like her either," Gertie said.

"Well, Jean's not exactly a little ray of sunshine herself." Aunt Rae carried her basket away.

Gertie didn't care whether or not Jean was a little ray of sunshine. She wouldn't want to be friends with a little ray of sunshine anyway. But she tried to think of something to say that would prove to Aunt Rae what a kind person Jean was. She thought and thought and thought. "Anyway—"

"Why do you want to be better than Mary Lou Spivey?" Aunt Rae used her bottom to bump Gertie's door open.

"Mary *Sue* Spivey."

"Well." Aunt Rae dropped a pile of laundry on the bed. "Why do you want to be better than her?"

Gertie knew that her aunt wouldn't like this mission, because she didn't like anything that had to do with Rachel Collins. Whenever Gertie or her father even mentioned Rachel Collins, Aunt Rae's nostrils would flare, and she'd heave herself off the sofa with a *humph* and start cleaning the house so violently that Gertie felt sorry for the dirt and grime. Gertie decided it wasn't a good idea to tell Aunt Rae about her mission.

"I just want Ms. Simms to like me," she said instead. "I don't think she likes me at all."

Gertie followed her aunt into the living room. Aunt Rae reached over the back of the sofa and tickled the bottom of Audrey's foot, which made her shriek and flail, which gave Aunt Rae a chance to steal the remote. She turned the TV off.

"I'm sure your teacher likes all her students equally," Aunt Rae said.

"I don't want her to like us all equally," Gertie said. "I want her to like me most."

"Okay," Aunt Rae said. "I'm sure that she likes all of you just the same. Especially you."

But Aunt Rae was wrong.

5

Nope

GERTIE RESEARCHED HOW LONG IT TOOK PEOPLE TO SHOOT movies, and it was ages. Mr. Famous Film Director Spivey would be here for a few more *months*.

So she and Jean got to work, brainstorming ideas for how to keep Mary Sue from utterly ruining Gertie's mission. Because Phase One had failed, the second phase had to be postponed, which was frustrating because Gertie couldn't stand waiting. Now Gertie's blue notebook had an entire page of ideas, titled "The New Phase Two." She had to find a way to end Mary Sue's awful reign as the lip-glossed queen of Room 5B so that she could move on to Phase Three, becoming the greatest kid in the world. And finally Phase Four, returning the locket.

But so far for Phase Two, they had only come up with ideas they couldn't use. For instance, they couldn't mail Mary Sue to missionaries in Taiwan so she could learn about Jesus, because the stamps would've cost more than a year's worth of their allowances.

And they couldn't convince everyone that deep down Mary Sue was evil, because she had become the most popular girl in school. She was always talking about what Jessica Walsh was like in real life, which Roy thought was fascinating. And she was always wondering aloud whether or not Gertie had warts from touching frogs, which the other kids thought was hilarious. And she was always saying how at her old school she'd been a gifted-accelerated-exceptional student, which Ms. Simms thought was better than butter on toast and which made Jean come up with more and more dangerous plans for Gertie's notebook.

A week later, Gertie still didn't have a plan she could use. As she jumped down the steps of the bus, she saw a truck snuggled beside Aunt Rae's Mercury, and she froze. Her father's truck was home, which meant her father was home, which meant—

"You gonna get out the way sometime today?" the driver asked behind her.

Gertie ran across the scruffy grass, book bag bouncing on her back.

Before she'd even made it through the screen door, her father's voice was booming across the house. "Gertie's home! Hide your valuables!"

Then he stepped into the kitchen.

Frank Foy was tall and handsome. He had blue eyes and one gold tooth on the top, and when he picked her up she buried her face in the space between his collar and neck and breathed in the smell of outside air and bacon and Listerine.

"Is the rig in good shape?" Gertie asked.

"Tip-top." He put her down and bent to scoop her book bag off the kitchen floor. "Did you get in big trouble at school?" he asked, which was his special way of asking what she'd done that day.

"I saved Junior's life in PE," she said. "And Ms. Simms says we have to memorize all fifty state capitals." Which was something she knew a lot of adults couldn't do, because she'd quizzed the mailman, and he didn't know more than seven.

"Let's see," her father said as he reached in one of the cabinets and pulled out a box of crackers and a tin of sardines. "What about Kentucky?"

"I don't know them all *yet*," Gertie explained.

"Well, which ones do you know?" he asked, which was nice because it gave Gertie an opportunity to show off how many she had learned.

They sat at the kitchen table, munching on crackers until they ran out of states. Her father rubbed the back of his neck. "Aunt Rae tells me you've been having trouble with a new girl," he said in his talking-to voice.

Gertie jumped to her feet. She had been all nice and comfortable, thinking they were having a lovely conversation without Audrey butting in for once in her life, when really her father had just been working up to giving her a scolding. She should've known it was a trap. "Wait a minute," she said. "You were talking about me behind my back?"

"Yes," he said, "because we—"

"I can't believe it! You're not supposed to talk about people behind their backs!"

"—care about you," her father finished. "I'm sure you'd like Mary Lou if you would just give her a chance."

Gertie didn't understand how Aunt Rae and her father could be so sure that Mary Sue was nice when they didn't even know her name. "Mary *Sue*. And she's *evil*. And I'm the one who's met her, so I'm the one who knows."

"You're positive?" He raised his eyebrows.

"I am." She sat back down.

He leaned back, propping his chair on its hind legs. "Is anything else bothering you?"

"Nope."

He brought the chair legs down with a *thunk*. "Did you see the sign in front of her—in front of your mother's house?" He looked at his hands and then glanced up at her.

Gertie nodded.

"Do you have any questions?" her father asked doubtfully, like he was hoping she didn't have any questions because if she did then he'd have to answer them.

Gertie had a million billion questions, but her father was starting to look as forlorn as any lost bullfrog. "Nope."

He sighed. "Well, you ought to know that she's getting married and moving to Mobile."

"I know."

"Oh." He frowned. "How? Who told you?"

Junior's mama had been cutting Rachel Collins's neighbor's hair and the neighbor had said something to Junior's mama, which Junior had overheard, and he'd said something to Jean, and Jean had also heard something from her father, and Aunt Rae had been having a private phone conversation, which Gertie was not supposed to eavesdrop on but she couldn't help it because what if Aunt Rae was talking about her behind her back and how was she supposed to find anything out if she didn't snoop? "I have my ways," she said mysteriously.

"Are you all right?" her father asked in a quiet voice.

Of course she was all right.

It was just . . . It was just that it wasn't *fair.* Frank Foy was the most interesting person Gertie knew. He juggled squashes and onions in the grocery store. He read yellowed paperbacks that smelled dusty sweet. He had big forearms from working with giant wrenches on the oil rig. How come Rachel Collins hadn't been happy with him? She should have chosen him and Gertie instead of some stranger.

And Gertie was going to make sure she knew it. As soon as she came up with a plan to get Mary Sue Spivey out of the way.

6

Upset About North Dakota

"ALABAMA'S CAPITAL IS . . ." MS. SIMMS STARTED WITH AN easy one.

"Montgomery!" everyone shouted together.

Then she moved on to the other states, and nobody answered except for Jean. Jean was twelve for twelve. Gertie could tell Ms. Simms was choosing the tricky states like West Virginia and Missouri, but Jean shot out answers almost as fast as Ms. Simms could ask the questions.

"Jean the Jean-ius," Roy muttered.

Jean sat straighter in her chair, and the corners of her mouth twitched up.

"What's the capital of"—Ms. Simms glanced down at her book—"North Dakota?"

Jean took a breath and was already opening her mouth to answer, but then she stopped. Her teeth clicked together. Her eyes darted from side to side. Everyone was watching her.

"Bismarck," said Mary Sue.

Ms. Simms looked up from her book. "That's right," she said.

"I learned my capitals *last* year," Mary Sue said, and shrugged one shoulder.

"Wow," Roy whispered from the back of the classroom. "She's a *real* genius."

"With a *g*," said Leo.

Jean trembled beside Gertie. When Junior trembled he was a scared rabbit, but when Jean trembled she was a volcano about to blow. No one had ever beaten Jean to an answer. Jean was the smartest girl in the whole school.

Except that now Mary Sue was smarter. Mary Sue was the best at everything. *She* was the best fifth grader in the world, without even trying.

If only someone would beat her at something. If only someone could prove that the seat-stealer wasn't the smartest. An idea nibbled at Gertie, and she tightened her ponytail.

While the rest of the class ran for the buses and cars, Gertie pulled out all her books until the inside of her desk was empty except for broken bits of pencil lead and a collection of rocks from the playground.

Junior and Jean stared.

"Did you lose something in there?" Junior asked, leaning over and peering into her empty desk.

"I'm taking these home to read." She began stuffing books into her bag.

"Why?" Jean put her hands on her hips.

"I'm going to study everything we're going to learn this year," Gertie said. She couldn't believe she hadn't thought of this before. "And then I'll know all the answers to every question Ms. Simms can possibly ask. I'll learn it all this weekend."

"*You're* going to study?" Jean asked.

Gertie's fingers reached for her shirt collar. She could do this. She could do anything. "Yes," she said. "This is how I'm going to do it." She waved her blue notebook at Jean. She lowered her voice. "This is how I'm going to neutralize Mary Sue." And become the greatest fifth grader. All in one blow. This was even better than the summer speeches.

"B-but—I—" Jean stammered. "It won't work!"

"Yes it will." Gertie kept loading books. It would work. She could feel it.

"But—you—" Jean grabbed one of her own books and stalked out the door, banging into people as she went.

Junior leaned toward Gertie. "She's just upset about North Dakota," he whispered.

Gertie squeezed one more book into her bag. She still had a stack on her desk.

"I guess you won't be able to carry them all—"

Gertie slapped a science book against Junior's chest, and he grabbed it before it could fall.

"Take this," she said. She tucked the last two books under her left arm and then hoisted her bag up with her right. "Come on, or we'll miss the bus!"

"You don't even *like* studying!" Junior said as he followed her, ducking a football that two boys were throwing in the hall.

"I don't have to like it," she called over the shouts of all the kids pressing out the front doors. "I just have to be the best at it. I'm going to be the smartest person in the class." Gertie climbed the bus steps and let Junior squeeze past her into the window seat. "I'm going to know everything." She had a thought. "Oh my Lord,

I'll probably have to move up a grade." She leaned her head back against the bus seat, letting the screams and shouts of all the other bus riders fade away.

Junior's next words were muffled because he had pressed his forehead against the window. "This is the worst idea ever."

Gertie snapped upright. She pulled on Junior's shoulder until he peeked at her from the corner of his eye. She spoke in her lowest, most serious voice. "Junior Jr., do you think I can't do what I say I'm going to do?"

His eyes widened, and he shook his head hard. "Of course you can." He swallowed. "It's just . . . Why do you have to be better than Jean? What if she gets mad?"

"I'm trying to be better than Mary Sue," said Gertie. "Not Jean. Understand?"

Junior didn't answer.

"Jean wants Mary Sue stopped, too," said Gertie.

"Umm . . ."

"You'll see," said Gertie. "Everything's going to be fine."

* * *

When the screen door slammed behind her she didn't even wait to see if Aunt Rae was going to come greet her. She rushed past her father, who was peeling boiled eggs, and Audrey, who was digging through the pots-and-pans cabinet. She hurried past Aunt Rae, who was straightening the sofa cushions.

"Can't talk! Big big plans," Gertie yelled, and she burst into her room, slid across the comic books on her floor, and crash-landed on the bed.

Gertie's bedroom was her favorite place in the world. Her trash can had a potted fern in it. She had a globe on her dresser and a do-it-yourself bonsai in the windowsill. Glow-in-the-dark stars covered the ceiling.

She pulled her spelling book out of her bag, propped it open against her pillow, put her chin in her hands, and stared at the words. Normally, she studied her spelling words the night before she had a test. They looked different this far in advance. When she'd memorized them all she looked at the clock and saw that she'd been studying for only twelve minutes.

A week's worth of spelling done in twelve minutes! Gertie was amazed. Maybe, she thought, she'd been a wonderful student all along and just hadn't known it. She was going to devote her life to studying. She was going to skip two or three grades. She was going to go to college when she was twelve. Phase Two: Win a medal! With her brain!

She decided to work on her capitals next. She would write them down five hundred—no, a thousand times each! She was picking up her pencil when the door creaked open and Audrey slipped into the room.

"I'm busy," Gertie said.

Audrey came further into the room, right up to the bed, and put her face an inch from Gertie's. "I can't find the channel changer."

Gertie didn't look up. "No."

Audrey breathed orange-juice breath in her face. "Do you want to play house with me?"

"No."

"I'll be the mama and the daddy and the cat and the Ford, and you can be the little baby."

Gertie started to remind Audrey that she was too old to play the little baby, but that conversation would take forever. "I'm doing important work," she said. "And I don't have time to play."

"Can I have some work?"

"No. You don't get to have work."

"Why?"

"Because you're in kindergarten," Gertie explained. "It's not real school."

"Why isn't it real school?"

"Oh my Lord!" Gertie was never going to learn the capital of Montana if she had to explain all of life to Audrey. "Why don't you go watch your *Waltons*?" she asked.

"But the channel changer's gone."

Gertie slapped her pencil down and rolled off the bed. "Come on," she said.

They looked under the sofa cushions and on all the tabletops and in the sock drawers and behind the washing machine. Finally, Gertie found it. For some reason, Aunt Rae had put it on top of the refrigerator, which Gertie thought was a ridiculous place to keep the remote because they didn't even have a TV in the kitchen.

"Better leave that be," her father said as he walked through the kitchen with his toolbox. "Aunt Rae put that there for a reason." He stepped through the screen door.

Gertie put her hands on her hips and looked up at the refrigerator.

Audrey put *her* hands on *her* hips and looked up at the refrigerator, too. "Oh my *Looooord*," she said in the most melodramatic voice ever uttered by a human being.

"You think you're mimicking me, but you're not," said Gertie, "because I have never sounded like that in my life."

Audrey was looking at the remote control, far above them. "We'll never get it down. Guess we'll have to play house instead, huh?"

Gertie climbed onto the kitchen counter and carefully stood. She lifted the remote out of the gray dust fuzz on top of the refrigerator and passed it down to Audrey. Feeling like she might finally be able to get some work done, Gertie went back to her room.

The capital of Montana is Helena. Helena, Helena, HELENA, Helena . . . Gertie wrote it over and over until she'd filled a whole page. She frowned at it, trying to decide if it was good and stuck in her brain crevices. Helena was a nice name. She wondered if Ms. Simms's first name was Helena.

"Gertie Reece, what are you doing in there?" Her father knocked on the door.

Gertie's head fell against her book.

"Aunt Rae wants to talk to you," he said.

Technically, Aunt Rae was Frank Foy's aunt, but Gertie always thought it sounded strange when her father said "Aunt Rae." Old people weren't supposed to have aunts. Old people didn't need aunts.

"Why'd you let Audrey have that remote?" Aunt Rae called. "I'm coming in."

"Aunt Rae!" Gertie jumped up so that she was standing on her bed. "You're invading my personal space!"

Aunt Rae flapped her hand in a shushing gesture. "What are you up to?" She toed some of the comic books out of the way.

"Albert Einstein didn't have these kinds of interruptions!" Gertie protested.

Gertie's father leaned over Aunt Rae's shoulder. "So?" he asked.

"So I'm studying because I'm going to be a real genius."

Aunt Rae blinked at the sight of Gertie's bed, covered in books. "Oh. You're studying." Aunt Rae looked at Gertie and her schoolwork a little longer, like she was making sure the sight didn't shimmer away like a mirage. When it didn't, she blinked again. She looked at Gertie's father, who shrugged. "That's good, I guess." She rubbed her back. "I'll leave you to it."

She turned to go but then looked over her shoulder, frowning. "What *else* are you up to?"

"Honestly," said Gertie, "y'all act like you've never seen me study before."

* * *

Gertie worked until it was time for bed, and after her father read her a chapter of *Treasure Island* and tucked her in, she worked by flashlight. She worked straight through Saturday, copying out the states and capitals and memorizing science facts and doing math sets until the fingers on her right hand had gotten stuck in a claw and her stomach snarled and her eyes blurred from staring at words and numbers and her brain felt like it had been sat on. And then she kept working until she fell asleep again.

And in her dreams Roy Caldwell whispered, *Wow, Gertie Foy is a genius with a* g—*a capital* G.

7
With a *G*

"Gᴇʀᴛɪᴇ."

Genius.

"Gertie."

"With a *G*," she mumbled.

"Gertie!"

She moaned and peeled her face off page sixty-three of *Adventures in Reading, Grade 5*, which she had been using as a pillow.

Aunt Rae shook Gertie's foot. "Church starts in twenty minutes."

"I should be studying," Gertie said, stretching.

"No."

She had inherited her commitment to missions from

Aunt Rae. And Aunt Rae had only two missions in life. One was not to buy anything unless it was on sale, and the other was to drag Gertie to church on Sundays.

So Gertie decided not to have an absolute conniption today—she could use a break anyway—and hummed as she pulled her church dress over her head and blew the hair out of her eyes. She hummed as she watered her fern. She ran to the kitchen door and hummed as she tapped her foot to show her father and Aunt Rae that she was ready to get this over with.

"You look like you've been dragged behind a car." Aunt Rae shook her head.

Gertie lifted her chin and hummed even louder. She was much too happy to worry about whether or not she looked like she had been dragged behind a car. She hadn't read through every book, but she'd read through a lot. And her head was fuller than it had ever been before. At school tomorrow, *she* would be the one with all the answers.

"Isn't it a lovely day?" she asked in her most airy-fairy voice as she climbed into the backseat and wrapped her seat belt around herself.

Aunt Rae grunted, and tugged up her skirt's stretchy waistband.

Her father settled in the passenger seat. Aunt Rae gripped the steering wheel and frowned at the clock. Gertie pretended not to notice. Normally, Aunt Rae took the long way to church. But whenever Gertie made them late, she had to take the shortcut, which took them on Jones Street.

Aunt Rae clicked her tongue and backed the car out of the yard.

When they sped by the housiest house, Gertie saw the lights on and the cars parked in the driveway. The Sunshine Realty sign was taller than Gertie and had a giant dancing sun, so it was hard to miss. But Aunt Rae didn't even glance at it. Neither did Gertie's father.

The First Methodist Church was a giant brick building across the street from the First Baptist Church. Gertie and Jean always met on the steps of First Methodist and waited together until they saw Junior going into First Baptist, which was where he went every Sunday. He said it was just as boring as their church, but he always got finished ten minutes earlier.

Jean was already waiting when Gertie got there. "How much have you read?" she demanded.

Gertie sat on the top step and tapped her toes against the brick. "Enough," she said, not giving anything away.

Jean frowned. "How much *exactly*?"

"Almost half of *Adventures in Reading*, four chapters in math, twenty pages of science, and a little bit of social studies."

Jean crossed her arms and leaned against a column. Gertie could see her doing some kind of calculation. When she was done with her figuring, she said, "You can't become smarter than Mary Sue in one weekend. It's not only about reading books. You have to *be* smart, too."

Gertie's toes stopped tapping. "I'm smart!"

"You're *smart*," Jean said with a wave of her hand. "But you're smart in other ways. You're not smart at school."

Gertie was about to argue when Jean said, "There he is."

Mr. and Mrs. Parks and Junior jogged across the parking lot and up the steps. They were always late.

"One," said Jean.

"Two," said Gertie.

"Three," they finished together. "HEY, JUNIOR JUNIOR!"

From all the way across the street, Gertie saw Junior's face give an amused twitch. Or maybe it was more of a horrified twitch. It was hard to tell. Mrs. Parks waved at them, and Gertie and Jean turned to go into their church, which was full of noisy, bustling people gossiping before the service started.

"Besides, I don't see how studying helps your mission," Jean said. "I thought you were trying to be the best at something."

"I am," Gertie said. "I'm going to be the best student."

"You can't be the best one at school," Jean said. "That's what I do. Junior's the jumpy one. You're the loud one. *I'm* the smart one."

"I'm not the loud—" Gertie began, but a woman shushed her. "I'm not *only* the loud one," she said more quietly.

"I'm just saying," Jean said in a don't-get-all-upset tone, "that making good grades isn't easy. You're going to be disappointed when . . ." She shrugged.

Gertie stopped walking so suddenly she was nearly run over by the preacher. Jean hurried away to sit with her family, without even looking back.

Gertie couldn't believe it. Jean didn't think she could beat Mary Sue. She wanted to follow Jean and tell her that she was forgetting that Gertie always did what she said she was going to do. But Mrs. Zeller never let

Gertie sit with Jean's family because Gertie couldn't act like a respectable human being during the service. Mrs. Zeller moved her purse to make room for Jean, who stared straight ahead.

Jean thought Gertie was just the "loud one"? Well, okay, it was true that she never had been the smart one before. But that was why she *had* to do it. She had to be a whole new Gertie when she faced Rachel Collins.

She walked slowly to where her father and Aunt Rae were sitting. "Genius with a capital *G*," she said to herself.

8

That Superior Smoothness

GERTIE HAD NEVER GIVEN UP ON A MISSION, NO MATTER HOW difficult it was. She hadn't given up on her mission to convince the cafeteria to serve rainbow toast on her birthday, and that had been extremely difficult. She hadn't given up on her mission to steal a ride on Roy's unicycle, and that had seemed impossible. She wouldn't give up now.

"What is the capital of South Carolina?" Ms. Simms asked.

Gertie threw her hand up at the same time that Jean punched the air with her fist. Then she stretched her arm an inch higher.

Ms. Simms looked up. "Gertie?"

"Columbia."

"Georgia?"

Jean's arm bumped Gertie's on the way up. Junior cowered in his chair.

"Jean," Ms. Simms said.

"Atlanta." Jean smiled.

When Ms. Simms called out the next state, Hawaii, and looked up to see Gertie and Jean halfway out of their seats trying to get their fingertips a little higher, her eyebrows rose. "Anybody else?"

"Honolulu," Mary Sue answered.

Gertie dropped her hand. Jean's teeth clicked together.

Later, they got out their copies of *Adventures in Reading, Grade 5* and opened to a story about a girl who raised a family of ducks that waddled after her.

"Roy, would you like to read?" asked Ms. Simms.

Roy didn't look up from doodling on his arm cast. "No, ma'am. Thank you for asking, though."

"Roy!" Ms. Simms snapped.

Roy shifted in his seat and began to read, muttering more and more quietly and turning redder and redder until Ms. Simms called the next person in line. Gertie scooted to the edge of her seat, waiting for her turn, counting people and paragraphs to see which one she'd get.

"Okay, Gertie, will you read the next one?"

Gertie cleared her throat and sucked in a big breath. Then she began reading in a loud, steady voice like her father did when he read to her. She didn't stumble over any words.

When her paragraph was over she tried to keep reading—just sneak on to the next one—but Ms. Simms stopped her.

"Thank you, Gertie. Let's let Junior have a turn."

Last of all was Mary Sue, and she read like she did everything else—better. She read in a louder, surer voice than anyone, even Gertie or Jean, and Ms. Simms let her read two *pages*. Mary Sue had gotten to read *two whole pages*, and Gertie had only gotten to read one paragraph, which was only two squinchy inches. Two pages. Two *inches*.

Gertie watched the back of Mary Sue's head, and she wondered why some people read better and had yellow hair and got to wear lip gloss and meet famous people and sit in the front row. And she wondered why *she* wasn't one of those people.

Jean's elbow dug into her ribs. "See?" she hissed as they put their books away. "I told you."

"So maybe it'll take me two weekends," said Gertie.

Ms. Simms was sifting through her papers. "I need one of you to run this to the office," she said, and Gertie forgot about her mission and Mary Sue and Jones Street and everything.

She reached her hand so high that her bottom came out of her seat.

When Ms. Simms looked up, everyone's hand was in the air.

"I'll take it, Ms. Simms," said Ewan, pushing his glasses up on his nose.

Junior put his hand all the way up and then almost brought it back down and then pushed it up again, like he wanted Ms. Simms to choose him but hoped she would never actually look at him.

The school secretary, Mrs. Warner, had a sister who lived in Switzerland and sent her fancy Swiss chocolates wrapped in gold foil. The chocolates were piled in a glass bowl on her desk, and whenever students ran an errand to the office, she would let them pluck one of the chocolates from the bowl.

Every student at Carroll Elementary—even the ones who had never tried them—knew that they were the best chocolates in the world. Some people said it was the crackly gold foil that made them better, and some people said it was the ganache centers. The creaminess. The perfectly round shape.

"It's that they have that superior smoothness to them," was Roy's mysterious explanation, even though he had never touched a corner of gold foil because the only time teachers sent him to the office was to see the principal.

Ms. Simms looked around the classroom. Her eyes stopped on Gertie.

Yes, yes, thought Gertie. She had never been asked to take a note to the office. Never. And she had always wanted to. Not just to taste one of the chocolates and experience that superior smoothness, but because she would've done an amazing job taking a note to the office. She would've gotten notes to the office in record time. She stretched her arm. *Please,* she thought.

"Gertie, would you take this?"

Gertie couldn't believe it. Ms. Simms was trusting her with the note. Ms. Simms was sending her to the office by herself. A solo mission.

All the hands fell. Gertie stood. Maybe Ms. Simms *did* like her. Or at least this meant that Ms. Simms didn't hate her. She was going to get a chocolate—a gold-wrapped chocolate in the middle of the school day. *That* was what mattered. *That* would make it all worthwhile.

Gertie could feel everyone's eyes on her as she walked to Ms. Simms's desk.

"Ms. Simms," said Mary Sue. "Our housekeeper was supposed to bring my allergy medicine to school. I forgot to take it."

Distracted, Ms. Simms looked at Mary Sue.

"I need to pick up my medicine from the office." Mary Sue glanced at Gertie.

Gertie was so happy that she didn't even mind the idea of picking up Mary Sue Spivey's allergy medicine. *Yes, you seat-stealer,* she thought, *I shall bring back your allergy medicine, because I am kind and I am going to get a chocolate.*

"I can get your medicine for you," Gertie said to Mary Sue. She turned to Ms. Simms. "I can get the medicine, too," she said. "I can do anything."

Roy snorted.

"I think I should get it myself," said Mary Sue.

"Yes," said Ms. Simms slowly, "Mary Sue had better get her own medicine."

Gertie froze.

Mary Sue had better get her own medicine? As if Gertie couldn't get the medicine. As if she might mess it up.

"Mary Sue, you take this to the office and you can ask Mrs. Warner if your medicine's there. Gertie, how about you take a note for me next time?"

It took Gertie a long moment to understand that Ms. Simms was saying that she couldn't go to the office. Disappointment cracked open in her chest. She could almost taste the Swiss chocolate even as she was realizing that she wasn't going to get one, maybe *ever*, because what if there never was a next time? What if Ms. Simms never needed another note taken to the office?

"Teachers always let *girls* run errands," Roy complained.

Mary Sue stood and pushed her chair neatly under her desk before she went to get the note.

Aunt Rae had been wrong. Ms. Simms did *not* like all of her students equally, and she didn't like Gertie especially.

Mary Sue walked out of the classroom. Before she closed the door, she looked at Gertie and flashed a smile that showed all her even white teeth. Gertie looked around, but no one else had seen it.

She took a deep breath and walked all the way back to her seat, her knees shaking. Ms. Simms started teaching. Gertie couldn't listen, though. All she could do was think about Mary Sue's smile.

Mary Sue had looked like she'd known exactly what Gertie was feeling and it was what she'd wanted. Her smile had said that she knew about Gertie's plans, and she'd messed them up on purpose.

When Mary Sue came back from the office, Gertie saw a flash of gold in her hand, and she had an even harder time concentrating after that.

At recess, Mary Sue positioned herself on the swing set next to Junior, Gertie, and Jean. Ella Jenkins and June Hindman hovered around her.

"I never *bite* chocolates," Mary Sue said, and popped the entire Swiss chocolate in her mouth. "I let them melt."

Gertie looked away from Mary Sue and turned to her friends. "She did that on purpose. She saw that Ms. Simms was going to let me go to the office, and she whined about her allergy medicine. I bet she doesn't even *have* allergies."

"She's a goody-two-shoes," Jean said, shaking her head.

It felt good to be agreeing with Jean again. Jean and Junior had always helped with her missions before. After all, it was Jean who had distracted Mr. Winston at the bait and tackle while Gertie had liberated the crickets.

And she never would've sold the most Girl Scout cookies in her troop if Junior hadn't persuaded Mrs. Parks to let Gertie sell to all the ladies in the salon.

Junior smiled at his two best friends. "I don't like her either."

There had to be another way to defeat Mary Sue. They would figure it out together.

9

No Way You Could Be Born on Krypton

IN THE FRONT YARD OF THE HOUSIEST HOUSE ON JONES Street, the Sunshine Realty sign began to fade. The poplar leaves turned yellow and, one by one, peeled off the tree like pages from a calendar. And Gertie's father went back to the rig and came home and went back again. And Mary Sue became more and more popular. Until one afternoon, while Gertie was listening to Junior, their bus turned onto Jones Street and, from the corner of her eye, she saw people standing in front of the house.

Junior was saying, "There's no way you could be born on Krypton, but you *might* be bitten by a radioactive spider."

In the yard, a man with a bow tie was gesturing as two women looked up at Rachel Collins's house.

"So there's no point wishing you could have Superman's powers, but you could be like Spider-Man. Sometimes I wish I'd find a radioactive spider . . ."

Gertie had never seen the man with the tie or the two women before.

"But I hope it would bite me while I was asleep, because if I actually saw it . . ."

She leaned close to the window to stare at the people as the bus passed. While she watched, the front door of the house opened and a woman stepped out. "Oh my Lord."

It was her.

All her life, Gertie had collected pieces of her mother the way other people collected little spoons or bracelet charms or Jessica Walsh action figures.

When she was little, she'd found the locket in Aunt Rae's desk, and Aunt Rae had pretended not to know anything about it, but it had belonged to Rachel Collins. Aunt Rae must not have wanted Gertie to have the locket, because she'd put it back in her desk. But she didn't say anything when Gertie filched it a few days later.

And after she'd asked and asked, her father had driven

her to the house on Jones Street and they'd parked by the sidewalk and sat in his truck, sharing a package of peanut butter crackers and watching the house. "That's where she lives," he'd told her.

And once, at the Piggly Wiggly, Aunt Rae had stopped pushing the buggy, and Gertie had looked up. Rachel Collins was at the end of the row. She had glanced up and seen Gertie and Aunt Rae. She had stared at Gertie for the longest time. She'd started to raise her hand, like she was going to wave, but then she'd closed her fingers and put her hand down and pushed her buggy away fast, the wheels squeaking.

"That's her?" Gertie had asked. She didn't know how she had known. Maybe she just *knew* because maybe a person always recognized her mother.

"That's her," Aunt Rae had said. "Acting like she forgot we live here, too." Aunt Rae shook her head, talking to herself now. "I tell you what. If she thinks the Pig ain't big enough for the two of us, then she can hightail her little heinie right out of here, because I'm not leavin' without my BOGO ground round."

Now the bus was past the house and moving away, and the people were getting smaller, and Gertie pressed closer to the window, her breath fogging the glass as she stretched to get one last look. Then the bus turned, and they were gone.

Gertie squeezed her eyes closed, and she could still see them. Rachel Collins was stepping down the porch stairs, smiling as she walked toward the other women. Gertie added the moment to the collection of scraps and bits that she had of her mother. It wasn't like these moments were important to her. They weren't. It wasn't like she pulled them out and shined them all the time. She just picked them up and kept them. That was all.

"They're probably looking at the house," Junior said in a strained voice.

Gertie jumped. She'd forgotten about Junior and all the other kids on the bus. "You don't think they'll buy it, do you?" she asked. She was still leaning over him to look out the window.

"I don't know." Junior's neck was pink. He blew her ponytail out of his face.

"Did you see the sign?" she asked. "Did it say the house was still for sale, or was it . . . Did it say it was sold?"

"For sale," he said. "I think."

Gertie fell back against the seat. Junior wiped his hands on the front of his shirt like he was nervous, even though Gertie was the one running out of time.

"You can do it," Junior said, as if he'd been reading her mind. "You can still do something big, I mean. You can do it at Career Day."

"What's Career Day?" Gertie demanded.

"We got that note about it," said Junior.

"What note? I didn't get a note." Gertie was glad she could be angry about something that was easy to put into words. The injustice of being the only one who didn't get this important note! Ms. Simms was giving notes to everyone but her, and maybe that was because she didn't want Gertie to have a chance at Career Day. It infuriated her. She was furiated, and it felt good.

"Everybody got a note," said Junior.

The first-grade boy in the seat in front of them turned around. "I didn't get a note," he said.

"No," said Junior, "it's for the fifth grade. Everybody in fifth grade got a note."

"Not everybody," Gertie said, "because *I* didn't get a note." She ripped open her bag and dug through her things. "Don't you think that's *wrong*?"

"Yes, but—"

"Don't you think that's mean?" She wanted to hear Junior say that Ms. Simms was being horribly mean to Gertie, because she was.

"Yes, but—"

Under her copy of *Adventures in Reading, Grade 5*, she found the remains of a note on school stationery. It was crumpled and covered in something orange and sticky.

"Yes," said Junior, "that looks like the Career Day note."

Gertie wasn't able to read all the words through the orange sticky stuff, so Junior told her what it said. The fifth graders were each supposed to ask an adult to come to school, and they would explain this adult's career, and it was supposed to help all the students decide what they were going to be when they grew up. Career Day sounded like the best thing Gertie had ever heard of.

"You always do good at speeches and things where everybody's looking at you," Junior said. "So maybe once you've given your speech you can tell her about it. I mean, she'll be proud, right? Your mom?" Junior's eyes were wide.

Gertie leaned toward him. "I don't want to make her proud," she explained. "That's not what it's about. It's about making her realize I'm important."

"Oh," said Junior, nodding. "That's okay, too."

* * *

When Gertie got home she collapsed onto her bed. The edges of the glow-in-the-dark stars blurred against the ceiling. She dangled the locket in front of her eyes.

Her father was back on the oil rig, so he wouldn't be able to come to Career Day in person, physically, himself, but that was okay. In fact, it was better. This way, Gertie would give the speech and explain her father's career all by herself. She was a capable and independent woman.

Her father spent two weeks on the oil rig in the middle of the ocean. He did everything on the rig. He worked, ate, slept, even played video games with the other workers. Then he got to come home for two weeks. Gertie loved when he came home because he'd missed her so much that he'd grab her arms and swing her around in circles through the air. And then he'd have to go away again.

It was dangerous work, so her father had to be very brave. And it was hard work, so he had to be very strong. Oil rigging was pretty much the weirdest, most wonderful job in the world. Which was why everyone else was going to be blown out of the water by her Career Day speech. Unless . . . unless Mary Sue brought her movie director father.

No, thought Gertie, that wouldn't happen. She just had to think positive.

She pulled out her blue notebook and wrote *Phase Three* at the top of a page. Ms. Simms would be stunned when she realized what an amazing public speaker Gertie was. She'd make all the other teachers come to listen. *Oh my stars,* they'd say to one another, *such poise, such a voice, an inspiration, a marvel!*

10

Who Wants to Go Next?

"Give 'em hell, baby!" Aunt Rae called as Gertie barreled out the screen door the next morning.

Gertie stomped through the crunchy leaves and up the bus steps, her Career Day speech clenched in one fist, her Twinkies in the other, not suspecting anything unusual. She barely noticed the thoughtful way the bus driver munched his toothpick as he gazed into his rearview mirror. She almost didn't hear the whispers as she ran down the aisle to her seat.

But when she reached her seat, she jerked to a stop so fast her tennis shoes squeaked against the rubber floor. Junior sat with his arms crossed over his chest. His smile stretched almost to his ears. Gertie stared. Around her, the whispers rose in volume.

"What is that?"

"Why'd he do it?"

"He'll probably get *expelled* with that—"

Junior's hair was shaved to short stubble on the sides of his head, and he had a stripe of longer, gelled-up hair down the center.

"I call this," he told her, "the Riptide."

Gertie sat. She had never imagined that hair could be like *this*, that it could make feelings unfurl inside a person.

Junior's hair made her feel like snapping her fingers at the whole world—*mmm-hmmm, oh yeah*. The Riptide was the satisfying *snick* of roller skates over sidewalk seams. It was grape Popsicle, frosty from the freezer. It was seeing your own face reflected, small, in someone's sunglass lenses.

"Can I touch it?" she asked.

Junior's neck turned pink, but he nodded.

Holding her breath, she ran her palm lightly over the spikes. She let her breath out in a shaky sigh. "Wow. Junior, that's really . . ."

"I know." He looked as pleased as Gertie had ever seen him. "Mom did it last night so we could show it off today."

The Riptide really was the most amazing thing. It was better than anything she'd ever imagined. A cloud passed over the sun, and the color faded out of the world. She tore her eyes away from Junior and slowly traced her finger across the names graffitied on the seat in front. Even her very exciting speech wouldn't be enough to beat the Riptide. But this was Junior Jr., and he was carefully running his hands along his buzzed head, so she made herself smile and pat his arm.

"You're going to be great," she assured him in the brightest voice she could manage, hoping Mary Sue wouldn't ruin it for him by bringing her dad and a couple of movie stars.

When Gertie and Junior walked into the classroom, everyone rushed over to examine Junior's hair up close. It was impossible to get enough. A person didn't want to look away from it. So many students stared at Junior's head that Ms. Simms asked him to sit in the back of the class so that the others would be able to focus on their work.

When the first adults started arriving, the students were so excited that Ms. Simms abandoned the lesson altogether and allowed them to greet each new person who walked in the door.

Mr. Zeller showed up wearing his uniform that said Zeller's Carpet Cleaners on the back. He stuffed his hands in his pockets and inspected the giant *Look What We've Accomplished!* board that Ms. Simms had set up. Gertie wondered if Mr. Zeller was counting the gold stars on Jean's homework assignments.

Gertie studied all the parents, matching them to the students. She was looking for someone who looked like he might be a famous movie director. Instead, a tall woman in a pale pantsuit waved to Mary Sue from the back of the classroom where the parents all crowded together.

Gertie knew then that Junior would be the best. And maybe she would be a close second, which wasn't enough, but she had to act like it was okay for Junior's sake.

Everybody demanded that Junior and his mother stand up first. They went to the front of the classroom. Mrs. Parks winked at Gertie. Nobody would have thought that skinny, nervous Junior was related to Mrs. Parks, who was plump and pretty and always had a calm smile. Junior rubbed his shoes against each other, but he was grinning.

"I'm Junior's mama," Mrs. Parks said, even though almost all of them knew her from years and years of haircuts. "I'm a hairstylist. It's a very exciting career because *this*"—she gestured at Junior's head like she was displaying a fantastic game-show prize—"is the kind of work I do at my salon."

Junior shoved his hands deep in his pockets.

Mrs. Parks said, "For only fifteen dollars, ladies and gentlemen, you, too, can have your very own Riptide."

The class gasped. Gertie hoped Aunt Rae would give her fifteen dollars.

The other parents glared at Mrs. Parks and shook their heads.

Her smile grew brighter. "I'll see you all after class." She and Junior went back to their places.

The students clapped and pounded their fists on their desks. One thing was for sure, thought Gertie. Mary Sue Spivey might have had the best of everything else, but at least she wouldn't have the best Career Day speech.

The other Career Day adults were nothing compared to Mrs. Parks. June's aunt was a dental hygienist, and she gave them each their own new toothbrush and a packet of floss and told them if they didn't use them she would know. Roy's father did something with numbers that even Roy didn't understand. Then it was Mary Sue's turn. She and her mother went to the front.

"Hello, children," said Mrs. Spivey.

"I know everyone wanted to meet Jessica Walsh and hear about the film," said Mary Sue, "but my father is very busy with—"

Mrs. Spivey put an arm around her daughter's shoulders. "I'm an environmental lobbyist," she said.

Everyone nodded, but Gertie bet none of them knew what she meant. Gertie thought of trees and clouds and hotel lobbies.

Mrs. Spivey must have seen their confusion. "That means I work with politicians. I ask them to pass laws that protect the environment. So our air and oceans will be cleaner."

People nodded. This was okay. It was no Riptide, but it was okay.

"What are you working on right now, Mrs. Spivey?" asked Ms. Simms.

"Since we moved here, I've taken a special interest in offshore oil drilling. I'm sure you've all seen the oil platforms off your coast. I'm working on ways to stop that."

Jean grabbed Gertie's arm. Gertie looked at her and saw that Jean was giving her a what-are-you-doing stare.

Gertie looked around in confusion and understood that, without realizing it, she had pushed her chair back from her desk like she was about to get up. She probably would have stood right then if Jean hadn't stopped her. She would have gotten out of her chair and . . . and . . . and she didn't know what. Leaving seemed like a good idea—walking right out the door. But running around the room and kicking things might also be a good idea. Since she couldn't decide what to do, she stayed in her seat.

She imagined the giant platforms that stood on stilts in the middle of the ocean. Why would anyone want to get rid of oil rigs? They were so *interesting*. Gertie had always been proud that her father worked on an oil rig. She'd thought about working on one herself one day.

Mrs. Spivey was still talking. "Well, those things are bad for the fish and the ocean. They're hurting our planet—"

In the back of the room, Mrs. Parks coughed several times. Ms. Simms frowned at her.

Mrs. Spivey went on. "So I'm trying to convince our representatives in Congress to pass laws to keep companies from building new oil rigs, and maybe one day we'll shut them down completely."

Gertie was observing the scene as though from a great distance. Mary Sue's mother was saying that oil rigs were bad things. She wanted to shut them down. If Mary Sue's mother destroyed all the oil rigs, then Gertie's father wouldn't have a job and he'd sit around the house all day getting sad and they wouldn't have any money except the teeny bit they got for babysitting Audrey and then they wouldn't have anything to eat and Gertie would be hungry all the time but she didn't care about that but she did care because her daddy would be hungry and Aunt Rae would be hungry and . . .

People shifted in their seats. Everyone knew that Gertie's father worked on an oil rig. Everyone except Mary Sue and her lobbyist mother. But . . . what if Mary Sue *did* know? What if she knew and she had invited her mother to Career Day on purpose?

Gertie could feel her classmates' eyes dart to look at her and then look away before she noticed. For once, Junior Jr. was perfectly still.

Jean nudged her leg under the desk. "Gertie," she whispered.

Gertie looked at her.

"It's your turn." Jean tilted her head toward the front of the room.

Even when she was standing up—even then—Gertie didn't know what she was going to do. She was like a thundercloud that gets fuller and taller and darker, lightning crackling on the edges, until it rips apart. She stormed to the front of the room. She turned around to face her classmates and their parents.

Jean leaned all the way forward toward Gertie so that she was lying on her desk like, if she could, she would jump over her desk and the front-row desks so that she could stand before the class with Gertie. Junior put his head down so that he didn't have to watch. He helmeted his hands over his head, crushing the Riptide flat. Gertie looked down at the speech she'd worked so hard on. The words were small and wobbly, and she couldn't read them.

"My daddy works on an oil rig," Gertie said, and she looked up, right into Mrs. Spivey's eyes. "Some people don't like oil rigs. People like *lobbyists*." She hoped she'd pronounced that right. "But without oil rigs, there would be no oil. Without oil there wouldn't be any gas for people's cars or for . . . ambulances."

Mrs. Spivey blinked several times, but Gertie didn't break her stare.

"Without ambulances there wouldn't be any way for

people to get to hospitals when they had awful accidents in their houses." She looked away from Mrs. Spivey and gazed at the rest of the class. Mary Sue glared at her. "So I think people who work on oil rigs are saving the planet."

The classroom was silent as she walked back to her seat and settled herself at her desk like she didn't have a care in the world. In front of her, Mary Sue's hands clenched into fists on her desktop.

Mrs. Parks lifted her chin and applauded, breaking the silence. Jean started clapping with her. Roy clapped twice, but he was laughing while he did.

Ms. Simms cleared her throat, and in a small voice asked, "Who wants to go next?"

11
Well Done, Gertie

AFTER HER CRACKLING, CATEGORY 5 CAREER DAY SPEECH, Gertie didn't think she'd have to worry about Mary Sue anymore. Not if Mary Sue knew what was good for her.

Now it was time to concentrate on what was really important, which was finding a way to show Rachel Collins that Gertie was the best thing that ever happened to Carroll Elementary School. But the next Monday, when Gertie stepped off the bus, the first thing she saw was Mary Sue and Ella putting flyers on the wall. They had already covered the front of the building in pink and yellow papers.

Gertie read the one that was closest. *Clean Earth Club, Recruiting New Members,* it said. *Don't believe what some people say. Learn the truth about offshore oil rigs.*

Gertie stared at the flyer. Was Mary Sue calling her a liar? She hitched her backpack higher on her shoulders and marched up to the two girls.

"What—what—" She was so angry she didn't even know where to start. "What in the Sam Hill are you doing?" she said in her most dangerous voice.

Mary Sue and Ella ignored her.

"What do you mean *some people*?" Gertie asked. "What do you mean *Learn the truth*? I told everyone the truth!"

Mary Sue rolled her eyes. "You said all that because you don't know any better. You're so ignorant." She pursed her lips. "I think we need one here," she said to Ella, and pressed her finger against the wall. Then, with a violent snatch, Mary Sue ripped off a length of tape.

Ella passed her a flyer.

Breathing like she'd just run a race, Gertie made herself squeeze her backpack straps and hurry down the sidewalk so she wouldn't do anything she'd regret.

She was *not* ignorant or stupid, and she would prove it. With or without Jean's help, she would show everyone that she was smarter than that lying seat-stealer. Gertie scraped her ponytail up to the very top of her head for maximum brainpower, and she started to study again.

She studied harder than she ever had in her life. She studied for days and then weeks.

Until one November afternoon, Gertie was holding her breath and crossing her fingers while her teacher swept around the room, dropping test papers on desks. Most people stuffed their tests into their books before running out of the classroom to wait for the buses and car pickups. Roy grimaced at his grade and rolled his test into a tight scroll that he used to whack people as he left the room. At least he didn't have his cast anymore. When he had whacked people with that it had hurt a lot.

Then Ms. Simms dropped Jean's test onto her desk, and Jean leaned over her paper so Gertie couldn't see. But by craning her neck and grabbing Jean's hand and prying her fingers away from the paper, Gertie just managed to see Jean's grade: 97.

"Let go," said Jean, tossing her head so that her hair whipped Gertie's face.

A test paper fell in front of Gertie, and Ms. Simms's big neat handwriting jumped off the page at her. *Great job! 99.*

Gertie screamed. She clapped her hands over her mouth. She had never before made a 99 on a test. Ever. And it made her feel like a new person, like the kind of person who could make 99s on tests. Gertie pulled her hands an inch away from her mouth. "Oh my Lord."

Ms. Simms smiled. "Well done, Gertie," she said.

Junior was stealing glances at Jean and eating his own shirt collar. Jean stood up and slammed her chair under her desk.

"Of course, I made a one hundred on that test." Mary Sue's voice floated across the room from where she was standing by the cubbies, fastening her shiny silver coat buttons and talking to Ella.

Gertie's hands were still at her face. She lowered them slowly.

"Schools are much more advanced in California," Mary Sue said, then smirked at Gertie over her shoulder as she walked out of the room.

Gertie looked back at the 99 and the *Great job!* She wanted to rip the exclamation point off the page, brandish it like a sword, and chase Mary Sue Spivey down the halls. She stuffed her test in a book and banged the cover on it.

When she looked up, Ms. Simms was watching her.

Her teacher tucked a piece of hair behind her ear. "Gertie, may I speak with you," Ms. Simms said. It wasn't a question.

Gertie frowned at her friends. Junior shrugged to show that he didn't know what she wanted either. But Jean didn't even look at Gertie. She headed for the door, her back ruler-straight.

Gertie waited until everyone had left and she was alone with her teacher. She walked to Ms. Simms's desk, which was heaped with papers and calendars and referral slips and glue sticks.

Ms. Simms put her elbows on a stack of worksheets and folded her hands. "Gertie, is anything bothering you?"

Gertie stared.

Itchy tags in her shirt bothered her. Having to sit still in church bothered her. Audrey Williams plucking leaves off her bonsai tree to feed her imaginary friend bothered her.

But right now she wasn't bothered. She was panicked. She had sharp pains in her chest and maybe it was a heart attack and she was going to be the first ten-year-old in the world to have a heart attack and when the doctors asked what happened, she'd moan, weakly, *Mary Sue Spivey did it to me.*

Ms. Simms cleared her throat, snapping Gertie out of her daydream. "I've noticed that you're working harder than ever on your schoolwork," Ms. Simms said, "and I'm proud of you. But it also seems like something's upsetting you."

Of course, it wasn't some*thing* upsetting Gertie. It was some*one*. But Gertie couldn't tell Ms. Simms about Mary Sue. She wouldn't believe her. Mary Sue always pretended to be nice when teachers were around. Ms. Simms hadn't seen Mary Sue's smile when she'd basically ripped a Swiss chocolate out of Gertie's hands. She hadn't seen the scheming look in Mary Sue's eye as she broadcast to the whole world that she'd made a perfect grade on her test. Gertie felt she could bear it if her teacher *knew* how awful Mary Sue was, but Ms. Simms wouldn't believe her, and that made the whole thing even worse.

She shook her head.

"Is it about Career Day?"

"No!" Gertie said. Career Day was the *last* thing she wanted to talk about.

Ms. Simms sighed. "Okay, Gertie." She leaned back in her chair. "You know you can talk to me if you need to, right?"

Gertie nodded as she turned to go, but she knew she would never be able to talk to Ms. Simms.

Outside, kids were yelling and horns were honking and parents were barking orders. Gertie hooked her thumbs in her backpack straps and scuffed toward her bus. A flutter caught her eye. A new paper was taped to the school's brick wall. Gertie walked over to it.

The Clean Earth Club is having a party! the flyer said. *Refreshments will be served. RSVP,* the flyer said. Gertie's shoes were stuck to the sidewalk. The bottom of the flyer flapped in the wind. Students and parents were walking past the sign, glancing at it. Hot shame washed over Gertie, and without thinking about what she was doing, she tore the paper off the wall. She shredded the offensive paper into ribbons that floated to the ground in slow motion as if she were in a movie—no, a *film,* of course a film. The last shred fluttered to the sidewalk, and the clapstick snapped down on the clapperboard. *Cut!*

And Gertie knew that she was in trouble. Big trouble.

Mary Sue was standing still in the churning crowd of students. She looked from the ground to Gertie. Gertie was sure Mary Sue was going to punch her in the face.

That's what Gertie would've done to someone who ripped up her invitation. She braced herself.

But Mary Sue looked down at her invitation again. And then a smile flashed across her face so fast that Gertie might've imagined it. She must have imagined it because a second later it was gone, and two tears that sparkled like diamonds slid down Mary Sue's cheeks.

Gertie swallowed. "Mary Sue, I didn't mean—"

Gertie didn't have time to say whatever it was she hadn't meant because suddenly *everyone* was there.

"Aww, don't cry." Roy tucked his football under his arm and patted Mary Sue on the back. He looked at Gertie like he'd never seen her before.

Gertie felt her shoulders pull up. "I—" They needed to understand that *she* wasn't the mean one here. That it just looked bad. That she hadn't meant to do it.

"I'll come to the party, Mary Sue." Ella turned to Gertie. "What did you do to her?"

Everyone was saying at once that they would become Clean Earth Club members. They all stood behind Mary Sue and glared at Gertie.

"I didn't . . . I . . ."

Someone was tugging on her sleeve. *"Gertie,"* whispered Junior. He pulled her back. "Let's go, Gertie."

12

There's *Right* and
Then There's *Right*

AUNT RAE SAID THAT SOMETIMES YOU HAD AN AWFUL, HOR-
rible, rotten day and you were sure that nothing was ever
going to be right again, but then you had a good sleep
and the next morning your Twinkies tasted creamier
than ever. And everything was okay. Or at least not as
bad as you had thought. Sometimes you realized it was
all in your head. Sometimes you realized everything
was going to work out for the best, which was nice. But
this was *not* one of those times.

The next morning Gertie trudged through the kitchen,
dragging her book bag by its straps.

"Give 'em hell, baby," Aunt Rae said.

Gertie moaned.

When she got on the bus, everyone whispered and glared at her. Even the driver's toothpick pointed at her accusingly. *You,* the toothpick seemed to say. *You're the one who made that wonderful California girl cry.*

Her Twinkies tasted like despair, sort of sticky and empty at the same time, and the first-grade boy in front of her watched her take every bite.

When Ms. Simms began their math lesson, Gertie reached into her desk for her pencil. It was broken. She pulled out another pencil, and it was broken, too. Every one of her pencils was snapped.

"Ms. Simms," she said, "I don't have my pencil." Gertie could feel everyone watching her. "I must've left it at home," she said.

Ms. Simms sighed and found a spare one in her desk drawer.

Gertie bent over her work and tried to concentrate.

She was trying her hardest to do well at school, but whenever Gertie felt like she was making progress, something seemed to go wrong.

The broken pencils were just the beginning. Homework assignments went missing from her cubby. Her own cubby! When it was Gertie's turn to read aloud, Ella would cough and cough so that Gertie couldn't even read through one sentence. During tests, when Ms. Simms wasn't looking, rubber bands would sting the back of her neck.

At lunch one day, she was eating her pear salad at a table with Jean and Junior and glaring at a flyer for the Clean Earth Club that was taped on the cafeteria wall.

"*She's* the one who's doing this." Gertie stabbed a pear with her fork and pointed it at the flyer. "I can't prove it. But she's—"

"Gertie." Junior's eyes followed her fork, his eyebrows climbing up his forehead. "What's—"

"—doing something sneaky with her club." Gertie blinked. A wrinkled Band-Aid was stuck to the pear she was about to bite.

"*Yech!*" She shook her fork until the pear and Band-Aid flew off the tines and splatted against the wall.

Laughter burst from behind her, and she turned to see Roy and Leo bent double they were guffawing so hard. Ewan Buckley stood beside them. He pushed his glasses up on his nose and pulled up one pant leg. His permanently scraped knee was uncovered and oozy and had a distinctive Band-Aid-shaped pale spot. A shudder shook through Gertie's body like it was looking for a way out.

The Band-Aid peeled off the wall and dropped to the floor.

Jean snorted into her milk.

Gertie stared at her. "You're not on their side, are you?"

Jean shrugged. "Well, you know, Mary Sue is right about pollution."

Junior looked from one of them to the other. "Who can say for sure?" He gulped. "I mean, there's *right* and then there's *right*. And then there's right and . . . and *left* . . . and . . ." Junior's voice trailed away.

"You just have to be the center of attention, as usual," Jean said to Gertie.

"That's not true! That's not what this is—"

"If you want to be my friend, you won't try to be smarter than me. Friends don't do that."

Gertie looked at the wrinkled Band-Aid on the cafeteria floor. "I don't want to be better than you," she started to explain. "I have to . . . I have to because . . ." She took a deep breath. "Because I want to . . . because before my mother leaves I want to . . ." It was something that was perfectly obvious but very difficult to put into words.

Like trying to explain the meaning of toes to Audrey. "I want to show her I don't need her."

Their lunch table was a pocket of silence in the noisy cafeteria. This was where Jean was supposed to say she understood.

"But being the smartest is *my* mission," Jean said. "Being the smartest is important to *me*."

Gertie stared at her. She had just told Jean that she was on a very important mission, and Jean didn't care. Her best friend should have understood.

"We're always doing your missions. But what about what I want to do?" Jean slammed her milk carton on the table. "It's not fair."

Gertie swallowed. She hadn't known that Jean wanted to have her own missions. She would've helped Jean with her missions, even though they probably would've been really boring because Jean didn't have a good imagination like Gertie.

"Well?" Jean said.

Gertie didn't know what to say. "I would help you if—"

Jean's nostrils flared. "Do you want to be my friend or do you want to keep on with your stupid mission?"

Gertie reached for her locket. Best friends weren't

supposed to call your mission stupid. And best friends were supposed to be forever. "I'm not giving up," she said.

Jean did not tremble like a volcano about to blow. Instead, she went very still, and for some reason Gertie knew that was worse. Jean's eyes fell away from Gertie's face, and she stared at her lunch tray. Then she picked up her plastic fork slowly, like it weighed a hundred pounds, and she began to eat her lunch, chewing each bite a million times before she swallowed.

None of them said anything. Junior tried to pass Jean the maraschino cherries from his pear salad, but she ignored him.

Gertie poked her own fork through her food, looking for more Band-Aids.

13

People Are Fickle

"Aunt Rae!" Gertie yelled. "Aunt Rae!"

Aunt Rae hurried into the kitchen. "What's the matter?"

Gertie threw her arms around Aunt Rae's middle. "Everybody hates me."

Aunt Rae rubbed Gertie's arms like she was trying to warm her up. "Who hates you, baby?"

"Everybody!" said Gertie. "The thing is, they loved me. They *loved* me, but now they hate me."

Aunt Rae clicked her tongue. "What happened?"

Gertie stepped out of her aunt's arms and plopped into a kitchen chair. "I accidentally tore up an invitation—"

Aunt Rae's forehead wrinkled.

"—to Mary Sue's party."

"Gertie!"

"It was an accident! And honestly, Aunt Rae, it was a little thing." Gertie held her fingers apart half a smidge to show Aunt Rae. "I didn't do it to be mean. You've got to believe me. It's a horrible club party thing. And they've been all up in my cubby. Nobody would've gotten upset by a . . ." Gertie took a deep breath.

"Okay, okay! I believe you."

"You do?" Gertie looked up.

Aunt Rae nodded. "I believe you."

"Oh." At once the kitchen seemed less dingy. The pot bottoms gleamed a little brighter.

"So why does everybody hate me?"

Aunt Rae got a glass and filled it with water. "People are fickle." She set the glass in front of Gertie.

The word *fickle* sounded cute and wee, thought Gertie. It didn't fit at all. Her classmates were mean and awful and—

"What's fickle?" asked Audrey. She stood in the doorway. One of the many frustrating things about babysitting Audrey was that you couldn't have a serious adult conversation.

"*Fickle*," said Aunt Rae, "means they change their minds all the time for no reason at all. Like the children at Gertie's school. One day they like her, the next they don't."

"I don't think we should be talking about this in front of Audrey," Gertie said.

"Not the Waltons," said Audrey, shaking her head. "They like each other all the time."

"Oh my Lord." Gertie propped her head in her hand.

Aunt Rae fixed a glass of water for Audrey, too. "Your friends don't hate you, Gert. They're going through a phase. Audrey, what have you got all over your clothes?" Aunt Rae asked.

Audrey pulled her dirty T-shirt away from her body and examined the stains as if they were fascinating artifacts.

"So what do I do?" Gertie wanted to know. She was willing to try anything because she had to get back on track with her mission. She would try whatever Aunt Rae suggested. She drank some of her water to see if water helped anything.

It didn't.

"What do I do?" she asked again, when Aunt Rae just frowned and rubbed the side of her head.

"Did your mama send you with a clean shirt, baby?" asked Aunt Rae.

"Oh my Lord," Gertie said again.

* * *

Even though Jean wasn't speaking to her and people were fickle, Gertie would've been able to focus. She would've been able to concentrate on her schoolwork despite the broken pencils and stinging rubber bands. She would've been able to concentrate on planning some way to become the best fifth grader once and for all. She would've been able to concentrate, except for the fact that the only thing anyone talked about was Mary Sue's party.

They talked about the party in loud voices.

How Mary Sue had a *heated* swimming pool so that it was possible to go swimming in *November*. How Mary Sue's mother was hiring a professional caterer. How Mary Sue's house had a giant staircase, one with shiny wood banisters, perfect for sliding down.

And they talked about the party in quiet voices.

"Can you bring the posters?" Ella whispered to Ewan on Wednesday.

"Did Mary Sue tell you what she's planning?" Ewan asked Leo in a hushed voice during recess on Thursday.

On Friday, Roy pretended to have to tie his shoe right beside June's desk. He whispered out the corner of his mouth, "I got the jars for—"

"Shh! Don't talk about it here," June told Roy, and she glanced at Gertie. "At recess."

In the hall, Leo was walking by and started to lean toward Roy.

"It's fine!" yelled Gertie. "You don't have to whisper. I don't want to be part of your secret club!"

They looked at her like she was a dangerous maniac. Gertie glared back at them because she wanted them to know they were right. She *was* dangerous, very dangerous.

She pulled her locket out from under her shirt and held it tight in her fist. "It's fine," she whispered to herself. "It's just fine."

"You've got to go to that party," Gertie told Junior on the ride home.

Junior's feet started kicking the bus seat in front of him. "I thought we weren't going."

"*We* aren't," said Gertie. "I can't go. But I need to know what they're planning, and they'll never talk about their club in front of me."

"*I* can't go either!"

"Yes you can. You're going to be my mole on the inside." Gertie had learned about moles from television. The mole pretended to be friends with the villains and used a hidden microphone to report their nefarious plans.

"I know about moles," said Junior. "I saw a show about

a mole who pretended he was a criminal, and he got murdered and fed to a panther named Delilah."

They had seen the same show.

"That's not going to happen," said Gertie.

"It's not?"

"Do you really think Mary Sue has a panther named Delilah?"

He rocked from side to side. "You were supposed to 'Respond, Sir, Very Pronto,' if you were coming, and I didn't, so they probably won't even let me in."

"Of course they'll let you in. If you tell them you're fed up with me and you hate me, they'll let you in. And that's not what RSVP stands for."

Junior tilted his head. "What does it stand for?"

"Don't change the subject. They'll let you in. And they'll have cake."

"You think they'll have cake? It's not a birthday party."

The bus screeched to a stop to let a kid off.

"Of course they'll have cake. You have to have cake at any kind of party."

Junior stopped rocking back and forth. "I like cake," he began, and then bit his lip. "But they're planning something awful!"

"Shh." Gertie looked around to make sure none of the other bus riders were eavesdropping. "That's the *point.*

You have to find out what they're planning, because if it's something that'll sabotage my mission, we need to know. We need to know so we can stop it."

"It's probably a Grind Gertie into the Ground Gang," he said as the bus was stopping at Gertie's house. "And they'll have a Squish Junior into Juice Committee because I'm your friend."

The driver honked the horn.

"Junior," Gertie said, "please be my mole."

Junior put his shoes on the bus seat and folded his legs against his chest, making room for Gertie to slide past him and into the aisle. "What if I get scared?"

"Hey, Mayhem!" the driver shouted. "Your stop!"

She slung her bag over her shoulder and looked at Junior, scrunched in his seat, and she was sure he would get scared, because he was scared of everything, but she didn't say it.

"Junior Jr.," she said instead, "I believe in you."

His eyes widened.

When she got off the bus, she looked back and saw Junior watching her through the window. She dropped her book bag, snapped to attention, and saluted him.

He stopped chewing on his lip. He sat up a little straighter and raised his own shaking right hand to his eyebrow, and it looked, thought Gertie, almost like a proper salute.

14
Delilah

"My name is Parks," he said, bouncing his eyebrows up and down. "Junior Parks."

Audrey covered her mouth with her hand and shook with giggles.

"Shh!" Gertie looked around.

Junior's eyebrows dropped so low that Gertie worried they were going to fall right off his face. "I don't *feel* like a secret agent," he said.

"Why not?" asked Audrey.

Junior, Gertie, and Audrey were hiding behind a shrub outside Mary Sue Spivey's house, which was more like a mansion. Audrey's parents were having a "grown-ups only" weekend in Pensacola. Gertie knew that for

Mr. and Mrs. Williams, "grown-ups only" meant "Audrey-free." Gertie could've used an Audrey-free weekend. Especially *this* weekend.

Gertie peeked through the leaves. A car parked on the street, and Ella Jenkins clambered out, carrying a poster board.

"Okay," Gertie said.

Junior was holding on to the shrub like it was a life raft.

"What's the worst that could happen?" asked Gertie, patting him on the back.

"You could get caught!" Audrey yelled.

Gertie clapped her hand over Audrey's mouth. "Shh," she hissed. "Quiet as little church mice, remember?"

Audrey nodded, and Gertie turned back to Junior.

"Even if you get caught," Gertie said, "the worst thing that can happen is they make you leave and you come right back here to us and we go home."

Junior let go of the shrub and nodded.

"That's the worst that can possibly happen," Gertie said again.

And she believed that it was.

* * *

112

Gertie watched Junior walk toward the Spiveys' front door. He was twitching so much he looked like he was doing some kind of chicken dance. When he got to the door, he stopped and swayed on the spot.

Audrey breathed in her ear. "Why isn't he going in?"

"Come on. Come on, Junior." Gertie twisted a branch in her hands and willed Junior to keep moving forward.

Junior lifted his hand to the doorknob and then jerked it back like the metal had burned him. Then he straightened, ran a hand over his spiked hair, and pushed the door open. He was in.

"Yes." Gertie sat back in relief.

"*Now* what are we going to do?" asked Audrey.

"Now we wait for him to come back out."

"Why?"

"Because we can't leave him." Gertie wrapped her arms around her knees and watched the house.

"Do you think they have a clown in there?" Audrey was squatting on her heels, her knees tucked under her chin.

"It's a secret club," said Gertie. "They don't have clowns. They make plans to do something horrible to me to keep me from my mission."

"Oh," said Audrey, and Gertie thought that maybe

she'd be satisfied for five seconds at least. "What mission?"

"I'm going to be the best person in the entire fifth grade, okay?" said Gertie.

Audrey shoved her hands in the pockets of her pink windbreaker. "Why?"

"Little church mice," hissed Gertie.

Audrey glared, but she kept her mouth shut for once in her life.

Gertie watched the house and waited. Right now, inside that big house, Junior was convincing everyone that he hated Gertie, asking to join their club, and getting proof that they were the ones sabotaging Gertie's schoolwork. Then he was going to get out of there as quickly as possible and tell Gertie everything. Easy-peasy.

She waited. And she waited. Was this Phase Four or Phase Five? She waited so long that her legs got stiff and Audrey had enough time to stuff her pockets with leaves from the shrub, dig a hole, bury the leaves, and ask seventeen questions.

Gertie shoved her hands under her arms to keep them warm. A car *whooshed* by on the street.

"I'm going to go take a look through one of the windows," Gertie said at last. "You stay put."

"Aunt Rae said you had to take me with you," said Audrey. "She said you couldn't let me out of your sight."

"She's not your aunt," said Gertie.

"But I call her Aunt Rae."

"But she's *not* your aunt, so you should probably call her *Miss* Rae."

"She's not your aunt either. She's too old."

"I can't go around saying *Great-Aunt Rae* all the time," Gertie said. "It takes too long, and I've got stuff to do."

Audrey started to speak, but Gertie didn't let her get a word in.

"Take your jacket off," Gertie instructed, shucking her arms out of her own jacket. "Because it's bright pink and we're trying to be invisible," she added, beating Audrey to the *why*.

They tucked their jackets under the shrub, and Gertie grabbed Audrey's wrist. Keeping close to the wall, they tiptoed to the nearest window. Gertie lifted her finger to her lips. She heard laughs and shouts from inside the house. She peeked over the windowsill and jerked her head back down.

"What did you see?" whispered Audrey.

She'd seen June Hindman. She took a deep breath and peeked again. June, Leo, Ella.

No Junior. No Junior anywhere.

She made a follow-me gesture at Audrey and sneaked along the house until they came to a sliding glass door. A quick look told Gertie that it led to a bright kitchen that, thank the Lord, was empty.

"You stay right here," Gertie whispered.

Audrey shook her head.

"Stay," Gertie commanded.

Audrey's lip stuck out, but she crossed her arms and squatted.

The glass door was unlocked, and Gertie slipped into the kitchen and crept to a door that led to the rest of the house. For a moment, even though her heart was pounding, she felt like a real spy in a movie.

The house was full of noise. Television noise, laughter, talking, coughs, sniffs, papers rustling.

"Do you think I'm Jessica Walsh's type?"

Gertie jumped. Roy's voice had sounded close. She inched away from the open door.

"She's not that nice," said Mary Sue. "I mean, we're friends, but she's actually stuck-up."

If Mary Sue Spivey thought you were stuck-up, you must have your nose so far in the air that you could smell angel farts.

"But I'm just saying, if she had a type—"

"It doesn't matter," said Mary Sue, "because she's already gone back to California."

"Without telling me goodbye?" Roy said. "Will she come back?"

"No," Mary Sue said sharply. "My father's finished filming. He's already left. And I'll be going home soon, too. I can't wait to be back in a *real* town."

Mary Sue was leaving! Gertie almost clapped her hands together, but stopped herself at the last second. *Good,* she thought, straining her ears as she leaned toward the open door. *Sayonara, seat-stealer!*

The voices in the other room rose as everyone muttered about Mary Sue leaving and about not getting to meet Jessica Walsh.

"But you can't go away!" Ella cried. "We're best friends."

"Well, we may not leave *so* soon," said a woman's voice.

The lobbyist, thought Gertie.

"We haven't decided anything yet."

"Yes we *have*," Mary Sue said in a tone that would've gotten Gertie in a lot of trouble.

"We like it here." Mrs. Spivey went on as if her

daughter hadn't spoken. "My work really matters, and Mary Sue enjoys going to school with normal children. Isn't that right?"

"What other kind of children are there?" Roy asked.

Gertie had never thought she'd side with Mary Sue, but now she found herself hoping that Mary Sue would get her way and go back to California where she belonged.

She didn't hear Mary Sue's voice make any answer, though.

Come to think of it, she didn't hear Junior's voice either.

Gertie looked around the door for half a second. She didn't see Junior anywhere. Everyone in the living room was working on some kind of art project. Leo seemed to be painting a picture on a poster board.

What had they done to Junior? She imagined him tied up in the attic. Stuffed in a toilet.

"Can't wait to see her face when she sees this," said Ella.

Gertie decided she would send Audrey next door to call the police to report a missing person or maybe a kidnapping or possibly a murder.

"She's going to have a duck," said Leo.

This was no longer a gathering-information mission. It was a rescue mission. Gertie retraced her steps and sneaked back through the glass door. She whispered, breathless, "Audrey, I want you to run—"

Gertie froze, and it had nothing to do with the cold.

Audrey was gone.

Gertie slapped a hand to her forehead. She had lost Junior *and* Audrey. Aunt Rae was going to kill her. What would she tell Mrs. Parks?

She couldn't decide whether to be scared or angry. What if Audrey was in real danger, and it was all Gertie's fault? It would serve Audrey right if she were in real danger, because hadn't Gertie told her to stay right there? Poor Junior, poor scared Junior. How could he mess up the plan, when they had been over it three thousand times? This was all her fault.

Gertie stood outside Mary Sue Spivey's house and shivered, wondering what she should do. She shivered again, and then realized Audrey would've been shivering out here, too. She would've wanted to come inside. She was probably in the house getting warm.

Why, oh why, hadn't she let Audrey keep her jacket on? Gertie swallowed her fear, turned back, and entered the house again.

"Audrey?" she whispered to the big, empty kitchen. She slipped past the open door to the living room and sneaked down a hallway. A thick rug cushioned her steps as she went from door to door, slinking past the open ones and putting her ear to the closed ones, wishing and willing herself to hear Junior's and Audrey's voices. The rooms were huge, and the pictures and furniture looked like they belonged in a museum. Gertie wondered if Rachel Collins would've needed to go to Jones Street if Aunt Rae had had a house like this one. She pressed her ear to a door and heard footsteps coming.

Gertie ran. She opened the first door she came to, stepped through it, and pulled it closed behind her. She was in a big, dark closet.

"Hello?" called Mary Sue's mother from the other side of the door.

Gertie breathed into her hand and closed her eyes. A good spy wouldn't get caught.

"Must be the cat," Mrs. Spivey said to herself.

Gertie Reece Foy wouldn't get caught.

When Gertie heard Mrs. Spivey's footsteps fade away, she sighed with relief and took a step back, expecting to fall into a soft heap of coats. Instead, she bumped into a soft heap of *person*. Someone was in the closet with her!

"It's me."

"Junior!" Gertie rubbed her chest. "Oh my Lord! My heart. What are you *doing* in here?"

"Shh." Junior's breathing was loud in her ears. "H-hiding?"

"You've been in here the *whole* time?"

"Let's get out of here," said Junior, clutching her arm. "Please."

"No," said Gertie, shaking him off. "We've got to find Audrey."

"Audrey?" Junior squeaked. "You lost Audrey?"

"She lost herself!" Gertie whispered. "Oh my Lord. Oh my Lord."

Audrey lost. All of them in enemy territory. She had thought that the worst thing that could happen was Junior getting kicked out. She had been wrong.

"Come on," Gertie said, and opened the closet door.

She crept down the hall, now with Junior clinging to her elbow and tiptoeing behind her. Gertie led them into a dining room with a table big enough for twelve large people. Audrey wasn't hiding under the table. They looped around and ended up outside a room where Mrs. Spivey was tapping away at a keyboard. She didn't look up as they slid past the open door. Gertie's palms were sweating. She peeked into a second, smaller living room where a pair of small shoes was sticking up over the back of the sofa. Gertie's heart stuttered.

She hurried in, dragging Junior behind her. Audrey and a woman sat on the sofa, staring at the television. Gertie let out a sigh.

"I watch this show all the time," Audrey was saying.

The woman worked a piece of gum up and down, up and down in her cheek.

"I wish my family was like that," Audrey said.

"Audrey," whispered Gertie, "you were supposed to stay outside. I've been looking all over for you."

Audrey didn't look up from the television. "Got cold."

"Come on," Junior pleaded, still hugging Gertie's arm.

"Go play with the others," said the woman. "We're watchin' John-Boy."

"Who are you?" Gertie asked.

"Brenda." She cracked her gum between her teeth. "The housekeeper."

Gertie had thought that maids were supposed to wear black uniforms with frilly white aprons and little hats and say things in a funny accent like *'Ere are ze allergy tablets, my leetle pet.* But this maid wore jeans and tennis shoes and talked like anybody else.

"You don't look like a maid," said Gertie.

"Probably 'cause I'm a *housekeeper*." Brenda looked Gertie up and down. "*You* don't look like a happy little party guest."

"We're spies," said Audrey, without glancing up from the television.

"Spies?" Brenda cracked her gum again.

"Spies." Audrey nodded once.

"Listen at that," said Brenda, and she raised her voice. "Hey, Mrs. Spivey, we got us some spies in here!"

"No!" yelled Gertie and Junior together.

"What's going on?" Mrs. Spivey stood in the doorway, looking at the children and the housekeeper in confusion.

"Help," Junior squeaked.

Footsteps shook the house. Gertie took several steps back and tripped over a chair.

Mary Sue pushed past her mother. "What are *you* doing here?" she asked Gertie. "This is a club, and you're not invited."

"I was invited," Gertie said, because it was the only thing she could think of. She stood up straighter. "You invited the whole school. And I'm a part of the school. And it's my right"—she shook Junior off and raised a finger—"my right as a citizen to be here."

"Mary Sue," said Mrs. Spivey, "don't you think we have room for one more?"

"She didn't RSVP," said Mary Sue.

Gertie was going to say that she was just about to leave anyway, because it was a lousy party, when Jean pushed past all the others who had gathered to watch.

Gertie stared at her very own Jean, and all the air leaked out of her lungs. *Jean* was holding a large can that was covered in paper and had the words *Clean Earth Club* painted on it. A drop of blue paint slid down the can and dripped onto the white rug.

"Now, Mary Sue—" began Mrs. Spivey.

"Don't you get it? We don't want you here," said Ella.

But Gertie didn't care about any awful thing Ella said, because nothing could ever make her feel more horrible than seeing Jean standing in Mary Sue's mansion, staring at the blue paint on the floor.

"You'd better be nice to her!"

Everyone in the room turned to look at Audrey. She stepped in front of Gertie, put her hands on her hips, and glared up at everyone.

Gertie closed her eyes. *No, no, no.* She opened her eyes.

"One day," said Audrey, poking out her stomach, "she'll be the boss of all y'all. Because she's on a mission to be the best fifth grader in the world!" Audrey crowed the last part.

She looked around at the bigger kids and Mrs. Spivey and Brenda. Gertie stopped breathing.

Ella laughed. Roy and Leo. Mary Sue. They were all laughing at her.

"Oh, yeah," said Leo. "That'll be the day. Gertie's not the best at anything."

"See?" Mary Sue glared at Gertie. "She hates me because I'm better than her. She's jealous of me."

Ewan pushed his glasses up on his nose and shook his head at Gertie.

Gertie's ears were hot. She couldn't breathe at all. She saw dark spots. She saw a dark streak run across a shelf that was high on the wall. But the black streak must not have been a hallucination caused by oxygen deprivation, because it knocked a vase from the shelf. China smashed against the floor.

"Panther!" said Brenda.

Junior jumped a foot off the ground. "Delilah!" he yelled.

"Panther, get down from there!" said Mrs. Spivey.

A black cat leaped off the shelf and landed on Junior's head. He screamed. The cat's claws latched on to Junior's face and shoulders.

Mrs. Spivey and Brenda lunged at him, each one grabbing one of the cat's legs. The cat squalled. Junior squalled louder.

"Don't hurt him!" shrieked June. Maybe she meant Junior, or maybe she meant the cat.

Gertie gasped in a gulp of air and pushed forward. She grabbed another one of the cat's legs and leaned back, pulling with everything she had. The animal yowled and let go of Junior. It landed on the floor and streaked away.

Junior ran.

Gertie fled after him, not even knowing where she was going, following a yelling Junior as they burst through the front door and pounded up the sidewalk.

They were running for their lives. Lungs burning. Tennis shoes tearing into concrete. Until finally they stopped, panting. Gertie's eyes stung. She leaned against a light pole and put her hands on her knees.

"It was a cat," Junior said over and over. "C-c-cat cat cat."

Gertie nodded. She stayed bent over, catching her breath until she heard feet slapping the pavement. Then she stood to watch Audrey coming toward them.

Audrey was gasping for air when she finally caught up. "Whew," she breathed. "Whew! We showed them, huh?"

"No!" said Gertie. "We didn't show anyone!"

Audrey's mouth made a small round *o*, and her face wrinkled up like it did when her feelings were hurt. But *she* was the one who had messed everything up. She was the one who had told everyone.

"You ruin everything!" Gertie said. "No wonder your parents never want you around!" As soon as the words were out of her mouth, Gertie wanted to take them back. They were bad words. They were the wrong words.

Junior's skin went white beneath the red claw marks on his face and neck. Audrey's butt landed on the sidewalk.

Gertie knelt beside her. "Audrey," she said, "I didn't mean it." And she *hadn't* meant it, she really hadn't. The words that had come out of her mouth had been an awful accident. Like dropping your ice cream cone, like falling off your bike, or stepping on a cricket.

"I'm sorry," Gertie said.

Audrey held her knees as tears spilled over her eyelashes.

Gertie put her arms around her. Her hair smelled like apples. "I'm so sorry."

She hadn't meant it. But Gertie knew that this time no amount of explaining was going to make it better.

15

Oh, Junior

JUNIOR WAS HAVING WHAT AUNT RAE WOULD CALL AN EXISTENTIAL crisis.

"I've never felt so panicked," he said. "I couldn't do it. And I thought, *If I don't do this, then I'm the worst friend in the world.* And then I got panicked about being the worst friend in the world. And maybe you wouldn't want to be my . . ."

Gertie leaned her head against the bus seat and gazed out the window, not seeing anything. Maybe everyone at school would've forgotten what had happened. Maybe they'd forgotten about Gertie crashing the party. Maybe they'd forgotten what Audrey had said.

"I wanted to help you, but when I tried to walk in the room . . ."

FOR SALE BY

Sunshine Realty

555-6169

Gertie sighed.

"I just . . . I just . . . couldn't." Junior hung his head. "I don't deserve to wear a Riptide."

They rode in silence, Junior scrubbing at his hair, which was starting to grow out, and Gertie's hands clenching when they passed the house on Jones Street. *For Sale*, said the sign, *by Sunshine Realty.*

"I'm sorry."

"It's okay," Gertie said, even though nothing was okay.

The bus moaned to a stop in front of the school. Gertie had been staring out the window so long that she couldn't see anything beyond her own reflection.

"Oh no," said Junior.

"What?" Gertie blinked and rubbed her eyes until she saw what Junior was looking at.

Outside the bus, most of the fifth grade was in front of the school, bundled in coats, chanting and marching in circles around a card table that was set up beside the main doors. The front of the table had a poster that said *Clean Earth Club*. Stacks of pamphlets covered the table, and the three girls behind it—Mary Sue, Ella, and Jean—handed them out to people.

The kids on the bus didn't scramble for their bags like they normally did. They looked at the scene outside the windows. Their mouths hung open. The first-grade boy in the seat in front of them turned around to look at Gertie.

"They're gonna get you so bad," he said in a nasal voice. "What are you gonna do?"

Up front, the bus driver pulled his toothpick from between his lips and stuck it behind his ear. He shook his head and reached for the lever that unfolded the doors.

Most kids would have crawled under a graffitied, gum-studded seat. Most kids would've refused to come out so that the driver would've had to drag them off the bus. That's what they expected Gertie to do.

But Gertie was not most kids. She stood up and slung her bag over her shoulder.

"You aren't going out there, are you?" Junior's fingers touched the cat scratches on his face.

She pushed past him and walked down the bus aisle, ignoring all the children who were leaning to look out the window. She strode down the steps and into the horde of marching, chanting students.

The noise pounded against her eardrums.

"We need clean seas! We need clean seas!" they chanted.

Gertie's plan was to walk through the crowd and go into the building like she couldn't even hear them, like they weren't even there, but before she could take another step, a voice shouted.

"There she is!"

Ella pointed at Gertie. Then she snatched a pamphlet and waved it at Gertie so that she could see a drawing of an oil rig with a big red *X* scratched over it. For Gertie it was like that drawing wasn't just any rig. It was her father's. And Gertie couldn't ignore them anymore.

"You don't care about clean seas!" she yelled. "You're doing this to be mean! All of you!"

"Save the planet!" Mary Sue called to the crowd of students streaming off the buses. A few of the parents who were dropping their children off walked over to the table.

"Stop the drill-ing," Roy chanted into a megaphone. He pointed the megaphone into Gertie's face. "Stop the drill-ing!"

Gertie pressed her hands to her ears. Her father was a good person. If he were here right now, they would all see that. They would all know. He was a good person. They couldn't yell at him if they knew him.

But . . . but Jean did know Gertie's father. She had come over to Gertie's house and listened to Frank Foy's stories and eaten the fried pickles he'd cooked and gone to the beach with him. She knew what an amazing person he was, but here she was taking money from a kid and stuffing it into a can.

"Thank you for supporting the Clean Earth Club," Mary Sue said in a sugary-sweet voice.

"Stop the drill-ing! Stop the drill-ing!" The marchers turned around and started circling the table in the other direction.

"You're all . . ." Gertie grasped for a word bad enough to fit. "You're all FICKLE!"

134

Gertie had once thought that word sounded sweet, but when she spit it out at the members of the Clean Earth Club it didn't sound sweet at all. Leo's mouth fell open, and he stopped marching. June crashed into him, and Roy crashed into her, and the chanting cut off.

"We need to talk," Ms. Simms said to the class. Her voice was quiet and careful.

The children looked at one another.

Ms. Simms folded her hands on her desk. "Do you think it's nice to say that we should stop drilling oil when you know that Gertie's father works on an oil rig?"

The class was silent.

"How do you think it makes Gertie feel?" Ms. Simms asked. When no one answered, she said, "June, how do you think this makes Gertie feel?"

Gertie swallowed. Her feelings belonged inside of her and not out in the open with everyone prodding at them. Ms. Simms must hate her. Gertie stared at a spot on her desk.

"Probably it makes her feel embarrassed," said June, "that her dad's doing something so horrible."

Ms. Simms looked at June until she squirmed. "How else do you think she feels? Ewan?"

"I think she should feel ashamed. Because she's jealous. And because she thinks she's better than us."

Gertie bit her lip. She had always liked Ewan, even after the Band-Aid thing. At least he had never teased her like Roy did.

"And now we all know it," finished Ewan.

In the first row, Mary Sue turned and smirked at Gertie over her shoulder.

"I think," said Ms. Simms, "that if I were Gertie, your club would hurt my feelings."

No one said anything.

"Gertie, is there anything you want to say to the class?"

Seventeen pairs of eyes stabbed Gertie like pins.

Gertie lifted her chin. "My feelings aren't hurt."

Ms. Simms sighed. "I'm glad your feelings aren't hurt, Gertie. But all the same, I think the class should consider whether or not it's going about this club in the best way."

"She called us a bad word," said Ella.

"It started with an *f*," said Ewan, tipping his head back so he could peer through his glasses.

Ms. Simms blinked. "Gertie shouldn't have called you a bad word. But—"

"It wasn't bad," Gertie said, even though she'd meant

for it to be the most horrible, hurtful word in the dictionary.

"Yes it was! It was, too, bad," Leo interrupted. "I heard it."

"Quiet!" said Ms. Simms, abandoning her careful voice and switching to her I-have-had-enough voice. "What we're talking about now is what direction you think your club should take. And whether or not it might be better if you didn't discuss your club during school."

"Are you saying we aren't allowed to do our part to make the world a better place?" asked Mary Sue.

"No, I'm not saying that," said Ms. Simms.

"Wouldn't the world be a better place if nobody worked on oil rigs?"

Everyone looked at Ms. Simms.

Her eyebrows drew down. "Yes," she said. "I suppose, if that's how you want to look at it." She sighed and opened her desk drawer. "But you'll have to have club meetings on your own time and at your own place." She pulled out the school handbook. "You're not to engage in club activities on school property unless they're sponsored by the school."

Ms. Simms saw their confusion. "No more chanting and marching." The class mumbled. She dropped the handbook back in her drawer and slammed it shut. "Now take out your homework."

"It's always one person who ruins it for everyone else," whispered Ella.

As they unzipped their bags, the others grumbled and glared at Gertie like it was her fault they couldn't have their club anymore, when she hadn't done anything.

Her whole class hated her. Jean was sitting beside her, her arms crossed, acting like Gertie didn't even exist. And what if they were right? What if, thought Gertie, her father was destroying the whole planet and he'd lied to her about how wonderful his job was? What if she *was* stupid and wrong?

A knock on the door came just in time, making Gertie shake off her despair. She grabbed her locket. She was on a mission, she reminded herself. And she couldn't give up.

The door swung open before anyone could get up to answer it.

"Junior!" said Ms. Simms in surprise.

The bus driver held his toothpick in one hand and Junior's shoulder in the other. Junior's spikes stuck out in every direction, and his shirt was twisted. Gertie realized that she didn't remember Junior getting off the bus behind her. She also realized that he looked exactly like he'd been in the kind of struggle where someone drags you out from under a bus seat against your will.

The bus driver pushed Junior through the door. "One of yours, isn't it, ma'am?"

"Oh, Junior." Ms. Simms closed her eyes and rubbed her temples. "*Where* have you *been*?"

16
A Very Good Opportunity

ON THE FIRST DAY OF WINTER BREAK, GERTIE STOOD AT THE front window, propping her elbows against the sill and peering at the crumbly road with the faded yellow lines.

She sucked in a breath and then huffed it out onto the cold glass. She dragged her finger through the fog, making a heart. When that faded, she fogged up the glass again and wrote her name. Then the Zellers' phone number. She was writing the name *Rachel*, but before she finished, through the letters she saw the blue pickup truck slow down on the road. She lifted her fingertip off the window as the truck turned into the yard.

"He's here!" she yelled, and ran outside.

The moment her father stepped out, Gertie threw her arms around him, and he hugged her back so hard he lifted her off the ground.

"I've got something to show you!" she said when he put her back down.

He reached into the cab of the truck and pulled out his duffel bag. "You do?" He raised his eyebrows. "Is it a surprise?"

"Yes. And oh my Lord, you are going to *love* it!" she promised.

They went into the house, and Aunt Rae distracted everybody with what Gertie's father called "the usual."

Give me that bag and let me get started on your filthy, nasty socks and *How was your trip?* and *Did you hear that what's-his-name died last week?* and *Gertie, let the man breathe* and *The gutters need cleaning out again.*

But finally Frank Foy collapsed in the recliner. He cranked his footrest up and wiggled his socked toes in the direction of the artificial Christmas tree. "All right, Gertie Reece," he said, "where's my surprise?"

Gertie ran to her room and flung herself on her bed. She reached under her pillow and pulled out the newspaper. She ran back to the living room and flapped the paper at him until he took it. Leaning over his shoulder, Gertie pointed to a paragraph in the classifieds. She had circled it in blue ink.

"There," she said. "Right there."

"Truck drivers needed," he read. He glanced over the top of the paper.

Gertie nodded and waved for him to go on.

He lowered his eyes to the paper again and read, "Must have a CDL license. Fifty hours a week. Call Josh for more information." He looked up.

Gertie nodded.

He rubbed his chin. "Do we know Josh?" he asked.

She shook her head.

"Let me guess. You want a truck driver's license?"

"No! Well, maybe one day. But not right now. No. *You* can be a truck driver!" She clasped her hands together against her chest. "It's a very good opportunity."

He folded the paper and swatted her on the head with it. "Gertie, I don't want to be a truck driver."

"Why not?" She'd searched through all the classifieds, and it was the best job. She thought it would be nice to drive a truck. You could listen to the radio all day and wear sunglasses and slurp those drinks that had the good crushed ice.

"I already have a job."

She walked around him and sat on the edge of the coffee table. She leaned her arms on her legs and sighed. She'd hoped that he would go for the truck driver job without asking any questions. She looked at him. "But, Daddy, it's a bad job." She reached out and patted his knee.

"Says who?" He tossed the paper on the sofa.

"Everybody!"

He leaned back in the recliner. "What does *everybody* say?"

"Drilling for oil is dirty and bad," Gertie said quickly, like she was ripping off a Band-Aid.

"I see." He frowned and was quiet for a long time.

"Well?" she asked. "Is it true?"

He gazed at the tinsel-strewn tree. "Yes," he said.

Gertie squeezed her fingers together.

"It's true that sometimes—almost never—but sometimes, there are oil spills and lots of fish die and the ocean gets polluted. And it's true that oil makes fuel that people burn." A line creased between his eyes. "There are a lot of factors I guess," he said.

"So why do you do it? Why don't you be a truck driver instead?"

"Well, calm down. Drilling for oil isn't *all* bad. Do your friends ride in cars? Do their parents drive cars?" he asked.

Gertie shrugged.

He nodded. "They do, and when they do, they're

burning fuel, which is also bad for the environment. But they do it because cars get them to school and work and the grocery store and all the other places they need to go."

"Like the hospital," Gertie said.

Her father blinked. "Exactly," he said. "Cars would get them to the hospital if they needed to go there. That's a good thing. Right?"

Nothing in the world felt good to Gertie.

"And farmers use tractors to grow food. They've got to have diesel fuel for their tractors. And there are all kinds of products that you've got to have petroleum to make. We have to have oil to keep living like we do. At least until they invent something better."

"But wouldn't you rather be a trucker?" Gertie picked up the newspaper.

"No. I like my job."

"Why?"

"I'm good at it. And that makes me feel proud." He ticked off a finger. "The people I work with are good friends." He ticked off a second finger. "I make enough money that I can keep you and me and Aunt Rae fed, watered, dressed, and housed and still have some left over to buy things like comic books and bonsai kits." Three fingers.

"Everybody hates you," she said. "But if you'd get a new job, then they won't hate you anymore."

"Everybody," he repeated, and he put his footrest down and leaned forward, looking her in the eye. "Is this about your mama?"

"No!" Gertie said.

"Because *everybody* still won't like me if I become a truck driver."

"You don't know that! If you were the greatest trucker in the world, maybe she would like you."

He looked down at his hands for a long time, and when he looked up, he had sad eyes. "The people who love me, love me no matter what my job is." He shook his head. "I thought you knew better." He sighed. "Why don't you go to your room and think about it?"

"What?" Gertie froze. Her father had never sent her to her room before. She wasn't the kind of kid who got sent to her room. She was a good kid. How could he have forgotten that?

"Go." He pointed.

Gertie stood up and walked, stiff-legged, down the hall. When she got to her room, she slammed her bedroom door.

There.

If he had a problem with her slamming her door, he could tell her about it. He could come right up to her, and she would explain that it was her door and she could slam it if she wanted to.

No one came.

Usually, when her father's vacation time was over and he packed his duffel bag to go back to the rig, Gertie begged him not to go. Usually, she locked her arms around him so tight that he called her a bulldog on a car tire, a barnacle on a boat's butt. Usually, she begged him to take one last look at her loose tooth or her half-finished comic or her bonsai's fungus. Usually, she promised to miss him every second of every day. Usually.

He came into the kitchen with his duffel bag over his shoulder.

Aunt Rae's scrub brush swished across the dishes. "Gertie, your daddy's leaving," she said.

Gertie didn't look up from her Spanish homework spread out on the kitchen table.

"Gertie," Aunt Rae snapped, "your daddy's going away to work around the clock to put food in your belly and clothes on your back."

Gertie erased one of her answers.

She didn't need him to put food in her belly. After all, she could always eat Junior's lunch. And she didn't need clothes on her back. She'd heard about people who didn't wear any clothes at all. They went around utterly naked. They lived in places called nudist colonies where they used lots of insect repellent and—

"Say-goodbye-to-your-daddy-right-now," Aunt Rae said.

Gertie finally looked up from her homework. "Adiós, amigo," she said.

17

What Happens to the
Junk Food?

REALLY, IT WAS A GOOD THING THAT NO ONE LIKED GERTIE anymore. Because now that no one would bother her at recess, she had an extra twenty minutes every day to study. And it was *excellent* that she didn't have to worry about whether or not she was hurting Jean's feelings anymore. And she was glad Audrey was mad at her and wasn't begging her all the time to play house and find the remote. So much time to study. All alone. By herself.

It paid off, too, because the next time Ms. Simms passed back a math test, Gertie had gotten every single answer right.

Gertie looked up at Jean, who was working very hard to pretend that her former best friend wasn't sitting right beside her. Had she seen Gertie's test? Gertie cleared her throat. Jean shifted through her desk so that books banged and number twos clattered.

Gertie turned to her other side and pushed her test toward Junior. "I made a one hundred," she said. "Triple digits."

Junior looked at the test and then glanced over at Jean. His shoulders hunched.

"Did you hear something, Ella?" asked Mary Sue.

"No," said Ella, smirking. "I didn't hear anything."

Mary Sue turned around to look at the second row. "Jean, did you hear something?"

Jean didn't look up from her desk. "*I* didn't hear anything."

Mary Sue beamed at Jean.

Gertie had finally become the best at something, only it didn't matter because nobody cared. She glared at the back of Mary Sue's head. It felt like she'd been staring at that yellow head forever.

"No talking," said Ms. Simms as she glanced at the clock. "I want you on your best behavior."

Junior sighed and, with one finger, passed her test back to her. Gertie folded the paper.

Someone rapped on the door.

"Everyone," said Ms. Simms, "Mrs. Stebbins is coming

to talk with you. You will treat her with respect, like you would any other grown-up or guest in our classroom."

Ms. Simms didn't have to tell them to be on their best behavior.

Stebbins was the art, drama, and music instructor. No one but Ms. Simms had ever called her *Mrs.* Stebbins. She was just Stebbins.

She had pearl earrings, dentures, and a gray bun with lots of bobby pins poked in it. Everyone agreed that she'd been working at Carroll Elementary School for one hundred and seven years. Everyone did whatever she said because if she decided you were too much trouble, she would lock you in the art supplies closet and never let you out, not even if the principal told her to, not even at the end of the school year, not even if you had to go to the bathroom.

That was why, as Stebbins stepped to the front of the classroom and faced the class, no one was thinking about being rude to her.

Without so much as a *good morning*, Stebbins said, "We will be putting on a play."

Mary Sue's head snapped up.

"*Romeo and Juliet*!" squealed Ella.

"No," said Stebbins.

"Is it about ninjas?" asked Roy.

"No."

"Is it—"

Stebbins held up her hand. "It is about a girl named Evangelina Who Would Not Eat Her Vegetables."

Stebbins spoke about Evangelina in capital letters. Gertie ironed out the creases in her math test as Stebbins continued.

"A group of children will play the various junk foods that Evangelina likes to eat, and another group of children will play the healthy foods that Evangelina does not like to eat. At first, Evangelina will be happy with her junk-food friends, but then they will turn on her and make her ill. And then"—Stebbins sniffed—"when things are grimmest, Evangelina's mother, sick with worry, will arrive with the cast of vegetables and fruits and healthy foods and make Evangelina well again."

Evangelina. Gertie's heart leaped like a fish. *E-van-juh-leeena.* It had that ring to it.

The rest of the class muttered. Evangelina sounded like a good part. But all the rest of the play sounded like the kind of thing adults did to warp kids for life. Like when Aunt Rae showed Junior pictures of naked baby Gertie.

"What happens to the junk food?" asked Jean.

"The junk foods are thrown out with the trash." Stebbins pressed one of her bobby pins deeper into her bun. "Which is to say, they die."

Ms. Simms's eyebrows drew together, and she cleared her throat.

Stebbins ignored her. "I expect all of you to audition. The sign-up sheet will be posted in my room on my supply closet door."

Junior shivered.

"Who gets to be Evangelina?" asked Roy. He sounded panicked, and Gertie knew he was imagining the horror of standing in front of the whole school looking like a rutabaga. A kindergartner like Audrey might think it was fun to dress up as an onion, but the fifth graders would never be able to show their faces in public again. "I want to be Evangelina."

Mary Sue spun around in her seat. "Evangelina is a *girl's* name."

"We could change it to Evan," Roy suggested.

"Like Ewan!" said Ewan. "But with a *v*." He held up his fingers in a *v*.

Stebbins looked at Roy. "*Girls* will audition for the role, and I will choose the one who is most ap*t*"—her dentures clicked on the *t*—"to play the part."

"You always give the good parts to the girls," complained Roy.

Stebbins raised an eyebrow. Roy glared at her for a second longer. Then he crossed his arms and looked away.

Stebbins didn't bother to say goodbye to the students or Ms. Simms before she walked to the door, stepped through it, and slammed it behind her.

As soon as she was gone, everyone broke into conversation about who would play Evangelina and what kinds of costumes they'd have and whether or not there would be singing, which would be awful, because they hated singing.

"I guess I'll have to audition for something," Junior told Gertie at recess, "because Stebbins'll lock me up if I don't. But I won't be any good. I'll get stage fright for sure. So I don't know why I should even bother." Mrs. Parks had shaved off the Riptide, and he kept touching his stubbly head like he was reaching for something that wasn't there anymore.

Gertie was much too excited about the play to keep listening to Junior, so she went over to where a crowd had gathered around Mary Sue.

"The second most important thing to know about auditions . . ." Mary Sue's voice was high. Her eyes shone, and strands of her yellow hair stuck to her lip gloss.

Roy and Leo had their heads together and were discussing ways they could make Stebbins's play less mortifying.

"We should have French fries falling from the ceiling and raining everywhere," Leo was explaining. He fluttered his fingers down to mime French fries raining down.

Gertie stepped closer to them and rocked forward on her toes. She wanted to squeeze into the crowd so bad that her fingers itched with longing.

"I hope there's a big fight scene," she said, in the same quiet, rushed tones that Leo had used. "Like a battle between the good and evil foods."

Roy's face lit up, his eyes far away, and she could tell he was already on stage, wrestling a healthful carrot to the ground.

"Yeah!" he began. "With forks and—" But then his eyes focused on Gertie, and when he realized who he was talking to, he turned away.

18
I Loathe Peas

THE FIFTH GRADERS HAD ART-MUSIC-DRAMA CLASS IN A ROOM
that was full of tables with mismatched chairs and
costumes with missing sequins and ancient art projects
that flaked paint and glue on the floor. Sometimes Stebbins decided to teach them art, and they colored with
broken bits of crayons. Sometimes she decided to teach
them music, and they sang "America the Beautiful" until
their throats were raw and raspy—no one ever dared to
ask for a drink of water. Sometimes she decided to teach
them drama, and they would play charades or pretend
to be jungle creatures or trees. Drama was Gertie's
favorite.

Today, Stebbins told them to sit, silent as their graves,

while she read them the script. Evangelina was sort of a whiny girl, but according to the script, she was beautiful, and when she got sick everyone was worried about her, which was lovely of them.

Gertie imagined herself on stage—thousands of people in the audience catching their breath as they saw Gertie-Evangelina growing sicker and sicker until an asparagus rushed onto the stage and saved her and everyone applauded and she smiled at them all weakly.

Stebbins's voice cut through Gertie's thoughts. "Now that you've heard the play, go sign up for the part that you will audition for."

The class raced for the sign-up sheet. Someone shoved Gertie into the giant papier-mâché duck propped in the corner of the room, so she was at the back of the crowd that pressed toward the door where the sheet was taped. June and Ella were in front of her.

"I'm going to try out for Evangelina," said June, standing on her toes so that she could see who was signing up, and so that all Gertie could see was June's thick braid.

"Oh," said Ella, and she lowered her voice. Gertie could still hear her, though, and she was pretty sure that everyone else in the room could still hear her, too. "Oh,

June, you don't want to do that. Mary Sue is gonna try out for that part. You know she'll get it. She's so pretty. It would be *so* embarrassing to try out for a part and then not get it."

June dropped to her heels. "Yeah. I guess she'll get it."

Gertie looked at the dingy toes of her tennis shoes.

"She's practically an actress already," said Ella, nodding. "I mean, her father's a director and she grew up with *Jessica Walsh*."

"Yeah." June's shoulders slumped, but then she smiled. "Hey! It'd be neat if she could get Jessica Walsh to be in our play."

"What?" said Mary Sue, and suddenly she was between June and Ella. "I can play Evangelina as well as she could."

June took a step back from Mary Sue and stomped on Gertie's foot. "I think it'd be neat if we had a famous person in our play," June said. "That's all."

Mary Sue rolled her eyes. "Being famous doesn't have anything to do with *real* talent." She turned her back to June.

Ella and June raised their eyebrows at each other behind Mary Sue's back.

"I'm going to try out for the Cucumber," Ella said at last, "because cucumbers are nice and slender."

"What does that leave for me?" June asked.

"The Squash?" Ella said.

Junior was standing at the supply closet door now, with everyone urging him to hurry up. He closed his eyes and jabbed his pencil at the sign-up sheet. It landed on the Potato, and he wrote his name in the space.

Roy was standing right behind him. He leaned forward so that his face was right beside Junior's ear. *"Meow."*

Junior jumped, his arms flailing, and his elbow slammed into Roy's nose.

Roy clapped his hands to his face. "Ahhh!"

The class pushed away from Roy and Junior.

"Wham!" yelled Leo. "Direct hit!"

Junior stumbled away as Roy yelled and held his nose. Stebbins appeared by Roy's side, and everyone fell silent.

She squinted at him. "It's not that bad."

Roy's eyes watered. "But—"

She rested her hand on the doorknob of the supply closet. The class shuffled back even further. "I've seen worse," Stebbins said.

"You're right. It's not that bad," Roy mumbled, obviously thinking about the poor kids who were probably still trapped in there with old paint and construction paper.

Gertie was the last one to sign up. She looked at the sheet and at her classmates' untidy handwriting in different shades of ink or pencil beside roles like the Orange, the Banana, the Cucumber, Candy, Cola, Chips.

Only one person had signed up for Evangelina. Mary Sue had written her name in such enormous letters that the only space left in the column for Evangelina was no bigger than a pinkie nail.

Gertie twisted her pencil in her hands. She didn't want to be the Banana. She didn't want to be Cola either. But it *would* be embarrassing if she auditioned and didn't get a part. Then everyone would be awful to her about *that*. The audition sheet swam in front of her eyes.

"Of course, *Gertie*'s going to try out for the leading role." Mary Sue raised her voice so that everyone turned toward her. "After all," she said, laughing, "she's on a *mission* to be the best."

Leo snorted a laugh.

Gertie bit her bottom lip between her teeth, put her face an inch from the sign-up sheet, and squeezed her name into the teeny-tiny space beside Evangelina Who Would Not Eat Her Vegetables.

"You're going to look ridiculous," said Mary Sue. "Like usual."

* * *

Gertie was *not* going to look ridiculous, because she was going to practice being Evangelina every waking minute. She knew that to get the part, she would have to work harder than she'd ever worked before.

"I *love* Twinkies," she said to Junior on the bus the next morning. She shoved a whole Twinkie into her mouth. She tried to say, *I love sweets—I'm only ever going to eat sweets,* but her mouth was so full it came out, "Mwwah lug swees. Mwwah onee er go ee swees."

"Good," he said, rubbing the sleep out of his eyes. "Because I'm going to try out for the Potato, and I don't want to be eaten."

Whenever Gertie fell or stumped her toe or got a twinge, she clutched at her stomach and said, "Oh, Mother, I feel terrible!" which was what Evangelina said when she got sick during the play's grimmest part. And she practiced swooning and collapsing onto a stack of sofa cushions until she got so good at fake swooning that she didn't even need the cushions. She could fall right on the floor without hurting herself.

Phase Number Whateverwhatsit: Become an acting *sensation.*

After practicing all afternoon in the front yard, she swept into the house, threw her coat off, and plopped into a chair just in time for supper. Aunt Rae spooned a heap of peas onto Audrey's plate and then took the pot over to Gertie's side of the table. Gertie tensed.

Aunt Rae dipped the serving spoon and then tipped it so that the juice strained off and started to move toward Gertie's plate. "Here we go—"

"No," said Gertie-Evangelina, throwing her hands up

as if she were warding off something so disgusting she would be blinded by the sight of that much awful. "I don't like peas."

That didn't sound right. It wasn't Evangelina enough. She tried again.

"I can't stand peas. I loathe peas. *Peeeeas—ahhhh!*" she yelled in horror, and pretended to be strangling.

After her choking and gagging had petered out, she lay with her cheek pressed against the table, tongue lolling, for five seconds. Then she sat up and pushed her hair out of her face.

Aunt Rae and Audrey stared.

"What in the Sam Hill are you doing?" Aunt Rae asked.

Audrey picked a pea off her plate and frowned at it like she was deciding whether or not she should bite it.

"I'm being Evangelina," Gertie explained. "She's the main character of the play. Everyone loves her. She doesn't eat peas or any other vegetables."

Aunt Rae dumped another spoonful of peas onto Gertie's plate so violently that pea juice splashed Gertie's face. "*I* don't like her very much." She beat the spoon clean against the edge of the pot.

Gertie wiped her face and sighed. "Aunt Rae, *everyone* loves Evangelina," she explained. "She's beautiful and interesting and she gets sick. But it's okay because in the end her mother feeds her all these vegetables."

"Humph." Aunt Rae wasn't happy. "What will your *father* say when I tell him you're refusing to eat your supper?"

Gertie pushed her peas around her plate. "Evangelina doesn't have a father," she said. At least Gertie didn't think she did. Stebbins hadn't said.

The pea pot slammed against the table. "*You* have a father, and he's working right now on an oil rig."

Gertie smooshed her peas with the back of her spoon.

"You look at me."

Gertie dragged her eyes up.

"You're so busy wanting what you haven't got," said Aunt Rae, "that you don't properly appreciate what you do got." She shook her head. "I know you have more ideas than all the rest of us put together, but they aren't all good ideas, Gertie." She stormed out of the kitchen.

Audrey leaned forward and whispered, "You don't want a daddy anymore?" It was the first time Audrey had spoken to her since Gertie had said the horrible thing.

"Of course I do," said Gertie. She wanted a father. It was just that she wanted a lot of other things, too.

She ate a bite of her pea mush. Maybe if she ate her peas, just this once, it would be like making it up to Aunt Rae.

"My mommy and daddy love me," said Audrey. She sounded like she was reciting a threadbare line from her favorite book. "And they want to be with me all the time, but they have to work sometimes." Audrey sat on her hands.

Gertie squished her peas against the roof of her mouth. *No wonder your parents never want you around* rang accusingly in her ears. She swallowed.

Aunt Rae didn't eat a bite of her dinner. She did laundry instead. Gertie didn't know how Aunt Rae had found so many dirty clothes. She wondered if her aunt kept an emergency stash of dirties for when she needed some laundry to slam in the washer.

When the Williamses came to pick up Audrey, Gertie watched as Mrs. Williams strapped Audrey in her car seat and Aunt Rae waved to them from the porch.

19

A Potato *Never* Quivers

GERTIE AND HER CLASSMATES WERE GATHERED IN THE AUDI-
torium, trying not to fidget.

"Roy Caldwell will be the Ham," Stebbins announced.

"What about the audition?" Roy asked.

Stebbins looked over the top of her clipboard. "No
one else wanted to be the Ham."

"Of course they didn't want to be the Ham!" Roy
jumped to his feet and headed for the door, waving his
arms. "It's a stupid part. It's not like the Ham gets to
destroy zombies or save the city from demon fire. Know
what the Ham does? Gets eaten!"

"Where do you think you're going, Mr. Caldwell?"

Roy answered over his shoulder. "This isn't a real
audition! I'm not missing recess for this!"

"Sit," said Stebbins, and her voice was soft as a lock turning over in a closet door.

Roy stopped. He shoved his hands in his pockets and glared at the floor as he walked back. He sat.

"Jean Zeller, you will be Cola." Stebbins continued down the clipboard, reading off the different parts and who would play them.

"That leaves," said Stebbins, "Junior and Leo, who will have to audition for the part of the Potato. And Mary Sue and Gertie will audition to determine who will be Evangelina."

Gertie watched Junior walk across the stage like a sailor walking the plank. He got to the middle of the stage and trembled.

Leo cracked his knuckles.

"Hold still," said Stebbins. She came down off the stage, turned around, backed up a few steps, and considered Junior.

Junior put his hands in his pockets and trembled harder.

"Hold still," Stebbins said again. "You are *quivering*. Jell-O quivers. A potato *never* quivers."

"He should *be* Jell-O," Ewan said.

"How could he make a costume for Jell-O?" asked June.

"It's better for you than ice cream," said Ewan. "That's what my mom says."

Stebbins put a hand to her forehead. "No, no, no." She pointed at Leo, who sat in the front row. "You will be the Potato."

"You will be . . ." Stebbins waved a hand at Junior. "Something else. Ask me later."

Then, just like that, it was Mary Sue's turn to audition. She handed Stebbins a big envelope.

"What's that?" asked Leo.

"It's her résumé and headshots," Ella whispered, as if anyone should have known that.

Mary Sue looked over her shoulder at Gertie. She studied Gertie for a moment, seeing that her hands were empty. No headshot. No résumé. Mary Sue raised an eyebrow.

Gertie bit her lip. Why hadn't she brought headshots? What were headshots? She gripped the sides of her seat and made herself watch as Mary Sue stepped into the center of the stage.

"Eat your vegetables, Evangelina," said Stebbins. She was reading the lines for Evangelina's mother.

Mary Sue lifted her chin. "No," she said in a voice that rang across the auditorium. "I will *not* eat my vegetables."

She stood tall and recited her lines. On stage, Mary Sue looked perfect. She had princess hair and pink lips and pale skin.

As always, Gertie looked exactly like herself, but for the first time, she wasn't sure that was good enough.

Gertie looked at the other fifth graders' faces and tried to tell what they thought of Mary Sue's audition. But they were whispering to their neighbors or winding bits of string around their fingers or drag-racing their jacket zippers up and down.

"Thank you," Stebbins said when Mary Sue had recited her last line.

Mary Sue flounced off the stage, not even glancing at Gertie when she passed her.

Gertie climbed the steps and walked to the middle of the stage. Overhead, the fluorescent light flickered. Her class was watching her, their legs swinging. The heels of their shoes *thump-thumped* against the chair legs. Gertie was trembling as much as Junior.

"Eat your vegetables," said Stebbins.

The silence stretched.

"Eat your vegetables," Stebbins said again.

Gertie swallowed.

Leo leaned over to whisper in June's ear. Mary Sue

smiled at Gertie. It wasn't a hello-there-friend smile. It was a hope-you-get-eaten-by-a-crocodile smile. Most kids would've melted into a puddle of woe. But Gertie was not most kids.

Stebbins clicked her tongue. "Miss Foy, if you—"

"No," she said. "I won't eat my vegetables!" It was like the summer speeches. It wasn't what you said. It was how you said it. She squeezed her hands into fists and screwed her face up, stamped her foot, and shouted to the ceiling, "I *hate* vegetables! You can't make me eat them!"

"But you'll get sick if you only eat candy," warned her mother.

"No I won't!" said Evangelina. "Candy doesn't make me feel sick. It makes me feel wonderful!" She lifted her arms in the air, threw her head back, and twirled around on one foot. She flung herself on the floor and beat the stage with her hands and feet in the most spectacular conniption anyone had ever seen. She shoveled imaginary sweets into her mouth and rolled over on her back and made an imaginary snow angel in a pile of imaginary candy. She became fantastically ill. She almost utterly died from poor nutrition.

"The light!" she exclaimed. "I see a big beautiful light!"

That wasn't one of Evangelina's lines, but it should've been. She collapsed.

Stebbins didn't read the next line. The auditorium was silent.

Gertie opened one eye to see what was happening. Then she opened the other. Her classmates weren't playing with their zippers and fidgeting anymore. They stared at her, their mouths open. The pizzazzosity of Gertie's performance had short-circuited their brains. *Pop! Pow!*

Stebbins pursed her lips and pressed a sprung bobby pin back in place. "I think we have our Evangelina," she said.

"Oh my Lord, oh my Lord!" Gertie was bouncing up and down on the bus seat. The spring in the seat *eek, eek, eeked.*

"I can't believe it, I can't believe it," Junior was saying over and over.

But Gertie could believe it. She had worked for so long, and she had tried so hard to be the best in her class. It was like that book about that train with the face who tried and chugged and tried to get to the top of the hill, and it took him forever, and you thought he was never going to make it, but then he did, and it was like *whew-whee*. And it was like *I knew it all along*. And it was like punching your fists in the air before the roller coaster screamed down. Gertie was tip-top, and she wanted to stay there forever. She pressed her hands to her cheeks.

When Mary Sue had begged Stebbins to let her audition again, she had looked upset. Her face had scrunched up, and she'd grabbed handfuls of her yellow hair. She'd looked like she was in utter agony.

Gertie brushed the thought away. She had won the lead role in the play fair and square. She deserved it. She had worked so hard and, besides, Mary Sue was *not* a nice person.

"I can't believe it," Junior was still saying.

"Hey!" Gertie splayed her fingers over her chest. "I *always* achieve my missions, don't I?" said Gertie, said Evangelina, said the most amazing fifth grader in the world.

Gertie was so excited she almost didn't notice the bus driver turn onto Jones Street. She almost didn't notice the bus trundling toward Rachel Collins's house. But when the bus passed the house, her eyes turned toward it, like they always did. Because if Gertie was a mosquito, then that house was her Zapper-2000, and she wasn't able to resist it. Her eyes locked onto the place where Rachel Collins lived and the sign in the front yard. The sign that had started it all. It was gone.

A new sign was speared in the front lawn. *Sold.* The sign in front of Rachel Collins's house said *SOLD.* All capital letters. Red letters. Capital red letters.

S-O-L-D.

20
I Won't Tell

JUNIOR WAS SHAKING HER ARM, ASKING OVER AND OVER, "What are you going to do now?"

The words beat in her head like a *drip, drip, drip* from a leaky spigot. *What are you going to do, to do, to do?* She spent the rest of the ride that way.

When she got home, she trudged across the yard, pushed through the screen door, and shuffled to her room. She buried her head under her pillow. *What are you going to do, to do, to do?*

She was too late. The house on Jones Street was sold. Now it belonged to complete strangers. Maybe her mother was moving out right this very second.

What are you going to do?

She threw the pillow across the room. What she had to do was make sure Rachel Collins *knew* how amazing she was. She had to *tell* Rachel Collins about the play and about being the smartest and about everything. Right now.

Gertie hurried through the house and peeked in the kitchen. Aunt Rae was peering into the refrigerator. Gertie tiptoed past the kitchen door and crept to the coat rack. She zipped up her jacket. Her hand was shaking as she reached for the doorknob, her reflection strange and wobbly in the brass.

Behind her, the floor creaked. Gertie spun around. Audrey had two crayons stuck in her mouth like walrus tusks.

"Audrey!" She lowered her voice. "Go away."

The crayons fell to the floor, and Audrey looked at Gertie's jacket. "Where are you going?"

Gertie started to tell her it was none of her business, because Audrey was weensy, but she remembered Audrey crying on the sidewalk. She hadn't ratted Gertie out to Aunt Rae about what had happened at Mary Sue's party. Maybe she wasn't *so* weensy.

"Audrey, you can't tell. This is important. I got the part in the play."

Audrey's hands hung by her sides.

"You remember about the play?"

In the kitchen, a pot banged on the stove, and the radio clicked on.

Audrey nodded. "About the girl who yelled at her peas."

"Exactly. I'm going to go tell Rach—my mother—" Gertie took a breath. "I'm going to go tell my mother about getting the part." Now that the words were out of her mouth, they seemed real to Gertie. Going to see Rachel Collins wasn't an *idea* anymore. It was a fact.

"Oh." Audrey picked up her crayons.

"But you can't tell Aunt Rae. Because if you tell Aunt Rae, it won't happen."

Audrey nodded.

"It's important," said Gertie. "It's . . . it's my mother."

Audrey nodded again. "I won't tell."

And Gertie knew that she wouldn't because Audrey understood.

Gertie turned back to the door. She pulled it open, and stepped onto the back stoop. She jumped down the steps and crossed the crunchy brown grass and cut through the scrubby trees onto the edge of the road. She didn't look back.

Gertie walked and walked and walked. Where Gertie lived, people didn't just walk down the road like *la-tee-dah, howdy-doo*. Aunt Rae's house was on a back road where they didn't have things like sidewalks

and streetlights. Big trees leaned over the road on one side. On the other, a few dead cotton stalks rustled in the wind. Gertie kept her chin up and her arms swinging by her sides, and she took long steps like she had somewhere very important to be so that people driving by would think to themselves, *That little girl is going places,* and they wouldn't call the police.

Eventually, Gertie turned onto another road that had more houses on it. She would tell Rachel Collins that she was the star of the play. And she would drop the locket in Rachel Collins's hand, and her mother would be so regretful because she would think that Gertie was the most brilliant kid in the universe. And she'd know that she'd made a big mistake leaving Gertie and Frank, and she was making another mistake marrying Walter because anyone would be happy with Gertie for a daughter. Gertie walked a little taller.

When she turned again, she was on a proper street. Now she walked on sidewalks with houses all around. She could see her breath in the glow from the streetlights. It seemed much further to Jones Street when she wasn't riding in the Mercury or the bus. But she was glad that it was so far.

Gertie felt like she was earning everything good that was going to happen to her. Like the further she walked, the more she deserved. Like each step was a point, a coin, a gold star that she was earning and saving up so she could get the biggest prize of all.

She didn't stop until she was standing on the front porch and her finger was hovering over the doorbell.

A car passed, and a dog started yapping in one of the other houses on the street. She pressed the bell. The *dings* and *dongs* echoed inside the walls.

The door opened, and yellow light spilled out of the house. Rachel Collins was smiling.

21
It's at Six

RACHEL COLLINS WAS SMILING WHEN SHE OPENED THE DOOR, but then she looked down at Gertie. And the smile slid off her face.

"How did—" she began. "What are you doing here?"

"It's me," Gertie said. "I'm Gertie."

"Yes, I know who you are."

"Oh." Gertie took a breath. Now was her chance to tell her mother that she had done it. Fifth grade was a dragon, and she had beaten it like a piñata. She opened her mouth to say the words she had practiced a thousand times.

Only, every time she'd imagined this moment, the Rachel Collins in her head hadn't been a real person. She'd

been a half-formed idea of a person, pieced together with the bits of her mother Gertie had gathered over the years.

But *this* Rachel Collins, who was frowning and holding tightly on to the door, had brown hair, just like Gertie. And she had a pointy chin like Gertie. And she was standing so close that Gertie could smell her perfume.

"Huh . . ." said Gertie.

Slowly, her mother opened the door wider. The crease between her eyebrows dug deeper, but then she seemed to reach a decision, because she stood straighter.

"Come in," she said.

So Gertie stepped across the threshold and into the housiest house on Jones Street.

She looked around and saw that she was standing in a big entryway. The faded *For Sale* sign was propped against a wall. The sounds of clinking forks and glasses filled the house, and behind her, the door closed with a soft *click*.

Rachel put a hand on Gertie's shoulder and steered her down a wide hall and into the kitchen. The counters sparkled. An iced cake sat on a giant crystal plate.

It would've looked like a magazine kitchen except for all the cardboard boxes stacked in a corner. They were sealed with packing tape and labeled with marker. *Cookbooks. Cups. Tools.* Gertie turned away from the boxes and snuck a closer look at the cake. It said, *Happy Birthday, Lacy!*

"Who's Lacy?" Gertie asked.

Her shoulders tensed. She realized, too late, that she didn't want to know.

"I'm going to call your aunt," Rachel said behind her.

"No!" Gertie spun around. "Wait—"

"Shh." Rachel glanced at a door. A little girl laughed in another room, and Gertie's shoulders drew up even further.

"I came to talk to you, and Aunt Rae'll just . . ." Gertie began, but Rachel was already dialing the number.

Even though she was sweating in her jacket and her fingertips were tingling as if her mission was static in the air, Gertie couldn't help but admire how her mother punched the phone buttons with purpose. Rachel Collins was one of those people who made every action seem important. For instance, the businesslike way she put one hand on her hip and tilted her chin down while she talked into the phone.

"Hello? This is Rachel."

She looked strange in the kitchen, Gertie thought. Her

clothes were too nice, and her jewelry was too sparkly to do the kind of kitchen work that always left Aunt Rae covered in dishwater and flour.

"Yes, she's here," Rachel said. "Gertie's here. She just showed up." She paused. "Okay. Okay. I understand." Rachel put the phone back in its cradle and turned to Gertie.

"Rae says you've been gone more than two hours. She's frantic." Her eyes moved over Gertie's face like she was looking for something there—something besides a biggish nose and freckles. "She said she'd be here as soon as she could."

Gertie was running out of time. She squeezed her hands into fists. "I came here to tell you that I'm going to be in a play."

Rachel brushed a strand of hair out of her eyes.

"I got the best part," Gertie explained. "Evangelina." Only, it sounded all wrong when she said it. The lights were supposed to grow brighter and Gertie was supposed to grow taller and Rachel Collins was supposed to drop her mouth open in utter shock at the amazingness of it all.

Instead, the icemaker in the refrigerator door clacked and popped.

"Okay. Thank you for telling me?" Rachel said. It

sounded like a question. She didn't look impressed, and she didn't look regretful about leaving Gertie.

Gertie's fingers uncurled. It wasn't working.

She was supposed to give the locket back to her mother now. She reached for the collar of her shirt and felt the hard lump where the necklace lay beneath the fabric. That was the last phase.

But she couldn't do it. Because as long as she had the locket, it was like Rachel couldn't go. As long as the locket wasn't packed up in those cardboard boxes, she wouldn't be able to leave. Gertie let her hands fall and hang by her sides.

"Will you come to the play?" she blurted.

"What?" Rachel tilted her head. "I can't. I mean, I don't think that's a good idea."

"You can." Gertie hadn't planned on inviting her to the play, but now she knew. Rachel had to come. She had to get out of this house and come to Gertie's school and *see* Gertie as Evangelina. She had to *see* that Gertie was a star. Then she would understand everything. Then the mission would work like it was supposed to.

"I made a decision to leave years ago, and I can't change that now." Rachel shook her head. "Even if I wanted to."

Gertie's breath caught. Did that mean she *had* wanted to come back? "You didn't *leave* leave," she said. "You're right on my bus route."

Her mother pursed her lips but didn't answer.

"Rachel?" a man's voice called. "Rachel, where've you gotten to?"

"Just a minute!" Rachel called. She looked at Gertie. "I have to go. They drove all the way here for the party. I don't want to keep them waiting." She stood up straighter. "I at least need to be there for the candles. I'll be right back." She lifted the cake and hurried out of the kitchen, the heels of her shoes clicking on the hard floor.

Gertie stared at the door Rachel had disappeared through and wondered why she had left her here. Did she think Gertie would misbehave or have a conniption or something? Because she wouldn't. She could eat cake and sit at a table as proper as any adult. She should march right after Rachel and tell her that.

She went slowly to the door and pressed her ear against it, listening to the sounds of gasps and talk and shushing and singing. She pushed it open a crack.

Rachel's back was to Gertie. A man—it must've been Walter—was holding his tie against his chest as he leaned over the cake, slicing it with a knife. Two little girls clapped their hands. And Gertie knew that one of them must be Lacy. They looked like a family, she realized. They looked perfect, like Audrey's Waltons.

Gertie had never liked that show.

Then Rachel Collins turned her head to smile at one of the girls, and without even thinking, Gertie stole a tidbit to add to her collection of things she knew about her mother: Rachel Collins was the kind of person who, when she smiled, had eyes that crinkled up at the edges.

Gertie backed into the kitchen, letting the door swing shut. She backed all the way to the refrigerator, and when her jacket bumped it, she slid down and sat cross-legged on the floor and held her chin in her hands, turning over the image of crinkled brown eyes. Walter had two little girls. Gertie hadn't known. Nobody had said anything about it. But Walter had two daughters, and Rachel Collins wanted them.

The icemaker made a low, steady whine, and Gertie dug her fingernails into her cheeks. And she waited because Rachel Collins had said she would be right back.

But she was still waiting when the front door slammed and the party got quiet. She pushed herself to her feet and went to the kitchen door. When she opened it, she saw

Aunt Rae, her gray windbreaker on inside out over her flowery housedress, stomping through the dining room.

Rachel put herself between Aunt Rae and her new family like she could shield them from the sight of her. "If you'll just come to the kitch—"

"You get yourself"—Aunt Rae put her finger in the middle of Rachel Collins's chest and pushed her backward—"out of my way."

Rachel sputtered.

"What's going on?" asked Walter.

Then Aunt Rae saw Gertie standing in the doorway between the kitchen and the dining room. She made a low sound and put her hand to her chest. "Let's go home, Gertie," she said.

Gertie walked through the dining room, past the staring girls, with her head as high as she could lift it. Slowly, she turned back to Rachel.

She didn't need a mother, she reminded herself. That was what she'd come here to tell Rachel Collins—that she didn't need anybody at all. But somewhere along the way, she'd started to *want* a mother.

"The play's in two weeks," she said. "That's a Friday."

Rachel looked at Gertie with the same expression she'd had when she'd almost waved in the grocery store.

It was like she was split into two people, one of them telling her to say yes and the other telling her to say no. And then she said it. She looked right into Gertie's eyes, and she said, "Okay."

"Who's that?" asked one of the girls. "Daddy?"

Gertie didn't wait to hear how Walter answered. She followed Aunt Rae out of the house. The Mercury was parked and running in the driveway. Audrey was strapped in the back. Gertie climbed into the front and wrapped her seat belt around herself.

"I was like church mice," Audrey whispered, her swinging feet kicking the back of Gertie's seat. "I didn't tell," she said when Gertie didn't respond.

"I know," Gertie said.

Aunt Rae settled into the driver's seat and held the steering wheel for a long time. The engine growled, and the vents blew hot air on Gertie's face. The Mercury's headlights shone on Rachel Collins's garage door until Gertie began to wonder if Aunt Rae was going to sit here all night. She glanced behind her at Audrey, who shrugged.

Gertie looked back at the house, and she realized something. "I forgot to tell her what time. She doesn't know what time the play is."

Aunt Rae finally looked up from the steering wheel. She grabbed the shifter and put the car into reverse. "It's at six," she said, without looking at Gertie. "Your play's at six."

They started to back down the driveway.

"Ahhh!" Aunt Rae shouted. She slammed on the brakes so hard Gertie's body whipped forward. Audrey shrieked.

"Lord have mercy!" Aunt Rae slung the shifter into park. She was staring into the rearview mirror.

Gertie twisted around and looked through the back windshield. In the weird red glow from the brake lights, Junior's eyes were enormous.

22

How *Will* I Carry On?

BEHIND CARROLL ELEMENTARY, ON THE PLAYGROUND, ON A swing, Gertie sat with her hands in her lap. She scuffed her shoes in ditches that had been dug deep by children's feet.

Junior whooshed past her.

"It was"—he swung backward—"so scary." He sailed forward, and Gertie's hair blew into her face.

Junior had already told her the story six times that day.

Yesterday, after he and Gertie had seen the awful *SOLD* sign and he'd made it home and gotten off the bus, he had been minding his own business—eavesdropping on the ladies who were getting their hair done—when the phone rang. His mom had answered it.

The first time Junior had told the story, he just said that his mom had answered the phone. The third time he told it, he added that her face had gone pale. This time, as he swooped past on the swing, pumping his legs, he said, "She gasped, and I knew immediately that something was wrong. I knew it."

"Hang on," Mrs. Parks said into the phone. "I'll call you back." She put the phone down and yelled, "Junior!"

She pushed him into one of the salon chairs and stomped the pedal, raising the chair until they were eye to eye. "Junior," she said, "do you know where Gertie is?"

"No," he said. "No, ma'am."

All the ladies looked at him over their magazines.

"Rae Foy just called." His mother grabbed the arms of the salon chair and held it still.

Junior hadn't realized that he was swishing it from side to side until she stopped him.

"She can't find Gertie," Mrs. Parks said.

"Gertie's missing?" Junior stared at his mom. *Missing.* Missing was bad. Missing meant gone. Missing meant kidnapped and cut to pieces and put in canned cat food. The hair-dye fumes burned his eyes.

"Did she say anything to you about running away?" his mom asked.

The women in the other salon chairs had put down their magazines and were leaning toward him, tugging their neck aprons off. "Oh, that child," said one. "Rae must be a wreck."

"No," said Junior. "She wouldn't run away!" She wouldn't run away from home without telling *him*. At least he didn't think she would.

"What happened at school today?" His mom never looked worried, but she looked worried now.

Junior tried to think. "We had auditions. She got the Evangelina part. I didn't get any part. I didn't even get the Potato."

She asked him who Evangelina was. She asked him question after question. But he didn't know anything, because it didn't make sense that Gertie could be missing. She wasn't the kind of kid who went missing. She was the kind of kid who rescued other missing kids.

His mother patted his knees. "Okay, baby. I'll call Rae back and tell her we don't know anything. Don't worry," his mom said. "She'll turn up. She's probably gone off on some crazy adventure and lost track of time. Don't worry," she said again.

She left and went back to the phone. She had forgotten to let the salon chair back down. Junior jumped out of the chair and staggered into a haircutting station. He went past all the ladies who were fluffing their curls and blowing their wet nails and talking about the Foys.

Junior shut the salon door behind him and collapsed on the stoop. His best friend in the whole world was missing. He laced his fingers between his knees. What if his mom was wrong? What if Gertie didn't turn up? And the worst part was that if she was really missing and gone, she would never get to complete her mission. She wouldn't be there to stop her mom from moving away. And . . .

And Gertie wasn't missing. She was still on her mission! She had gone to Jones Street to the house with the *SOLD* sign to see her mom and tell her that she was the greatest fifth grader in the world. And now everybody *thought* she was missing, when really she was just on her mission. Really she was fine.

Except, except . . . what if something went wrong? Always before when she'd done a mission she'd had him and Jean. And then she'd only had him. And now she didn't have anybody. What if she got lost? What if she got attacked by a rabid coyote? What if she got her foot caught in one of those drains under the sidewalk and she couldn't get it out and she fell in and nobody heard her yelling?

He leaped up from the stoop. He had to find her. He ran inside and got his coat. Then he ran outside. Then he ran back inside and got his flashlight and hurried back out.

What if he got lost? What if he got cold? What if he never found Gertie? But he had to stop worrying about himself and start worrying about Gertie. What if *Gertie* got lost? What if *she* got cold?

And he walked to the street and started down his bus route. "My name is Parks," he said to himself, *"Junior* Parks."

Junior always stopped telling the story at this point. His chest puffed up, and he swung so high that he looked like he'd shoot into the air if he let go of the chains.

"And then Aunt Rae almost ran over you," Gertie finished for him.

As the swing fell back, Junior dragged his heels in the dirt. He jerked to a stop. He gripped the chains and turned to look at Gertie. "Yeah," he said. "But the point is that if your aunt hadn't been there to almost run over me, *I* would've been there to take care of you. I did it." Junior smiled and began to pump his legs again, swinging higher and higher. "I feel like everything's going to be better!" he shouted. "From now on!"

And despite the fact that everything had gone wrong for *forever*, it seemed like Junior might be right.

For instance, Gertie was famous. Somehow, everyone knew that she had walked to Jones Street, and no matter how many times she tried to tell them that she hadn't run away from home, that was what everyone thought she'd done.

The first grader who sat in front of her on the bus gave her a quarter out of his lunch money. And Ms. Simms patted her on the back and told her that if she needed anything, to let her know. A sixth-grade boy asked for her autograph.

Ella Jenkins showed up at Gertie and Junior's lunch table and dropped her tray with a thud. "Tell me everything," she said as she peeled the lid off her pudding cup. "Were you going to live in the mall? Because if I ran away, I'd go to Pensacola and live in the mall." She licked pudding from the lid and sighed. "It's just so exciting."

Gertie knew that they were being fickle, which meant that sometimes they liked her and sometimes they didn't, so she ignored them.

She kept the quarter.

Another good thing was that it was only a week until the play, and Gertie was a spectacular Evangelina. Even June had said that she thought Gertie was a good Evangelina. And Ewan had asked her if she would rehearse with him. They were all so impressed with Gertie.

And Rachel Collins would be impressed, too, when she saw Gertie in the play. And she *would* see her, because Gertie had been standing right by the phone when Aunt Rae had called and in a gruff voice told Rachel what time to show up. It was all settled.

Her mother would know that Gertie was wonderful and amazing and that she'd been wrong to leave her. And Gertie would give back the locket after the play. And even if her mother still married Walter and went away to live with him and his daughters, at least Gertie's mission would be accomplished. At least Rachel would know.

She was on stage, tying Evangelina's pink hair ribbon around her ponytail. People were tap-dancing around the stage in their tennis shoes, making awful squeaking, thudding sounds. Junior was practicing with the curtain.

"Mary Sue Spivey, you will be the Kale," Stebbins said over the noise. "It's nutritious."

Ever since auditions, Stebbins had been assigning Mary Sue different parts, but she had refused all of them. Junior was in charge of raising and lowering the curtain, which was a difficult job since he'd broken one of the pulleys. Mary Sue was the only one who didn't have a part to play.

"I will not be the Kale," Mary Sue said now in a calm, dignified voice.

Everyone in the auditorium froze. Stebbins's eyebrows rose, and she regarded Mary Sue like she was wondering whether she should boil her or bake her. "Fine," she said. "You will help the third graders with the set design."

"I'm an *actress*." Mary Sue crossed her arms. "Actresses are *not* set designers."

Stebbins ground her dentures. Then she scribbled something on a sticky note, tore it off the pad with a flourish, and ceremoniously affixed it to Mary Sue's shirt.

Mary Sue tilted her head as she tried to read Stebbins's writing upside down.

Ewan squinted at the note. *"Under—understudy?"*

Mary Sue snatched the note off and read it for herself. Her mouth fell open. "I can't be the understudy! I'm—" Mary Sue started to argue, but Stebbins turned her back on her. "Stop! Stop! You—you're—you're a—a horrible old woman!" Mary Sue yelled at Stebbins's back.

Junior gasped, and the curtain fell.

"Oh." Stebbins's voice floated through the curtain. "My feelings. They are so hurt. How *will* I carry on?" Her voice rose. "Mr. Parks, get that curtain under control."

When they began the rehearsal, Gertie-Evangelina pranced about and threw fits and pretended to be gravely ill while Mary Sue sat in the folding chairs with her hands in her lap and her eyes on the floor. Which was what she deserved, Gertie told herself. But for some reason, she found it difficult to prance and pretend to eat sweets while Mary Sue looked so squished.

Mary Sue was a seat-stealer, Gertie reminded herself. She was a horrible person, and everything was working out just like it was supposed to.

"Gertie, will you please take this to Mrs. Warner?" Ms. Simms asked during math class later that afternoon.

Gertie looked up from her math sheet. Mrs. Warner.

The secretary. Mrs. Warner was the secretary in the office. Ms. Simms was asking her—*Gertie*—to take a note to the office. She slid her chair back and put her trembling hands on her desk and pushed herself to her feet.

Jean glanced at her. Junior's mouth dropped open.

"Always the girls who get to take notes," Roy muttered.

This was it. She was *that* kid, the kid who got chosen to take notes to the office. She was the kid who would get a chocolate. The special kid, the something-extra kid, the eat-my-dust kid.

Ms. Simms handed her a note written in big, neat teacher handwriting. Gertie held the paper by the edges so she wouldn't smear the words. She walked to the door, feeling her classmates' eyes following her.

She skipped down the halls, the note waving from her hand. When she went by a classroom, she stopped skipping and walked, book-on-her-head straight, past the doors, like she was very grown-up, like *ooh-la-la* and *how-do-ya-like-that*, while her heart pounded from skipping.

Junior had been right. Things were going to be wonderful from now on. Oh, Junior was right about everything! She could've kissed him if he weren't . . . Junior.

Gertie got to the office in no time at all. She thought

about turning around and walking back to the classroom and then turning around and walking back to the office, just to make the whole experience last longer. But she wanted to do a good job, and she knew that Ms. Simms would think that doing a good job meant walking the note to the office only once. She pushed through the door.

The printer spat out sheets of paper, and Mrs. Warner's fingers clacked away on a keyboard, and on the desk sat the glass bowl of Swiss chocolates.

Gertie placed the note right beside the chocolates.

"What've we got here?" Mrs. Warner slid her glasses off her head and peered through them. "Approval forms," she muttered. "Signatures."

The phone rang.

"All right," she said, picking up the phone. "Thank you, dear." Mrs. Warner wedged the phone between her cheek and her shoulder. Then she waved her hand at Gertie as if she were shooing a fly.

Gertie didn't move.

"Carroll Elementary," said Mrs. Warner in a bright voice. "Louise speaking."

This wasn't how it was supposed to go. She was supposed to get a chocolate now. She had delivered her note—she hadn't even walked down the hall twice—and now Mrs. Warner was supposed to pick up a gold-foil-wrapped chocolate and drop it in her palm. If she didn't, then Gertie would have to walk back to her classroom *empty-handed*. Everyone would ask where her chocolate was and what did it taste like, and when they realized that she didn't get one, that she was the first person ever to take a note to the office and *not* get a chocolate, they would know she was . . . was . . .

The printer groaned and clicked and chewed up a sheet of paper.

The chocolates were waiting. Gertie was waiting. Mrs. Warner swiveled in her chair to examine the printer.

Gertie gulped in a breath through her mouth. She wasn't going to get a chocolate. It didn't matter that she was a state-capitals-and-math genius or that she'd gotten the best part in the play, because after everything Gertie had worked for, she still wasn't *that* kid—the kid who got the chocolate. She wasn't the kid who wore fancy lip gloss or had fluffy yellow hair.

Gertie turned away from the chocolates and started toward the office door. Lifting her hand to the doorknob took all her strength. She opened the door, but she didn't step through it.

Because, sometimes, a person just had to say *no*.

No. No, siree, Gertie Reece Foy wouldn't take it anymore. She. Would. Not. Take. It.

Gertie let go of the doorknob and turned back to the office. The secretary's wide back was to her. She was beating the printer with her fist. Gertie lifted the glass bowl off the desk, turned around, and walked out of the office.

23

Ger-tie! Ger-tie! Ger-tie!

WITH EVERY STEP GERTIE TOOK DOWN THE DESERTED HALL-way, the bowl of chocolates in her hands grew heavier and heavier.

What had she done? What if one of the teachers walked up and saw her? What if Mrs. Warner noticed that the chocolates were missing and she chased Gertie down and tackled her and chocolates went flying everywhere?

Gertie stopped walking. She was a *thief*. She was a *criminal*. Her whole future—down the toilet, floating with the goldfish and bobbing with the Barbie heads.

She started to turn around to take the chocolates back. But it wasn't fair! She had earned these chocolates fair and square. Who was the smartest girl in the fifth grade? She was. Who was the best Evangelina ever? She was. Who had delivered the note in record time to Mrs. Warner? *She* had!

But if she walked into the classroom with the bowl, Ms. Simms was sure to ask questions, and would she give Gertie a chance to explain? No way.

Gertie looked at the chocolates and tried to figure out what she should do with them.

One-handed, she stuffed her shirt in the waistband of her jeans. Then she pulled her shirt collar out and poured the chocolates down her front. The foil wrappers scratched her belly. She placed the bowl on the floor, right against the wall so that anybody who saw it would think to themselves, *Oh, here's a lost bowl,* and they wouldn't suspect a thing.

When she stood up, the chocolates rustled against each other and made a loud *shrr-shh.* She would have to walk very slowly so that she didn't rustle.

She opened the door and crept to her desk without looking at anyone. She sat carefully and picked up her pencil and started working on her math problems, but it was impossible to concentrate on math when she had a lifetime supply of chocolates in her shirt.

"Why are you lumpy?" asked Junior out of the corner of his mouth.

Gertie's ears burned. "You can't just ask a person that," she hissed. Now everyone was going to think she was lumpy.

"Why *are* you lumpy?" Jean whispered. It was the first time in weeks that she'd spoken to Gertie, but Gertie ignored her.

Numbers swam in front of her eyes. Her pencil scratched an answer that might have been right. The heater clicked on. An awful thought came to her. What if the chocolates all melted and got squishy and covered her shirt? And then Ms. Simms would want to know why she had brown lumpiness all over her?

Jean was eyeing her stomach. Gertie leaned forward to hide her lumpy middle. *Shrr-shh.* Junior jumped.

"Ms. Simms," whined Mary Sue, "I can't concentrate because it's so noisy."

Sweat slipped down Gertie's neck.

"Everyone, please be considerate," Ms. Simms said without looking up.

Gertie leaned over her work until her neck began to ache. But she couldn't move. If she moved again and Ms. Simms heard it, she would want to know why Gertie was rustling.

Taking the chocolates had been a bad idea. The only thing to do was eat them as fast as possible so that she wouldn't get in trouble. After what seemed like forty-five years, Ms. Simms announced that it was time for recess.

Gertie waited until everyone else had run for the playground before she stood up. Then she walked carefully to the very back of the playground where no one ever played. Junior followed her. She looked around. When they were alone, she pulled her shirttail out, and all the chocolates spilled onto the ground.

"Here," she said, tossing one to Junior. The chocolate bounced off his chest. "Help me eat these."

Junior picked up the chocolate and turned it over in his hands. "Where did . . . Oh no," he said. He dropped the chocolate. "Oh no, no, no." He took a step back.

Gertie's fumbling fingers tore the wrapper off one. She shoved it in her mouth and started chewing like it was her job.

"What were you thinking?" Junior put his hands on his head.

Gertie's cheeks were so stuffed she couldn't answer.

"What are you *doing*?" asked a shrill voice. Mary Sue had appeared from nowhere. She was standing behind Junior and staring at Gertie.

Gertie froze, but only for a second. If she ate all the chocolates, there wouldn't be any evidence. If she ate them all, it would be like it hadn't happened.

"Those are not your chocolates!" said Mary Sue. "Those are the chocolates for the good kids."

Ella ran up to them but skidded to a stop when she saw Gertie. "The Swiss chocolates!"

"Stop it right now!" said Mary Sue. "I'm going to tell." But she didn't move.

People began walking over to see what was happening, because the first law of the universe was that if you didn't want anybody around, *everybody* showed up. They shoved Junior aside and gathered around Gertie. She ate faster. She had to eat all the chocolates. If she got them all in her belly they would be gone, and if anyone said, *Gertie took the chocolates,* she would say, *Prove it.*

"The mother lode!" Leo said, seeing the pile of chocolates.

"Look at her," Mary Sue said to the others. "Look at what she's doing!"

"You're going to get it," said Ewan. "You're going to get it good." He shook his head. "And when I say *good,* I mean *bad.*"

"You really are Evangelina," said Ella. "All you eat is sweets."

Gertie was unwrapping chocolates and stuffing them in her mouth as fast as she could.

"I've never had one," said June.

"That's because those chocolates are not for everybody!" Mary Sue's face was turning red. "They're only for good kids!"

"*I'm* a good kid," said June.

"Ugh!" Mary Sue stamped her foot. "They're for important people. That's what I meant."

"Well, I've never had one," Leo said. "Does that mean *I'm* not important?"

"That's not what I meant!" said Mary Sue. "You're making this all wrong. She's messing everything up!" She pointed at Gertie.

Gertie put her hands on her knees and leaned over, breathing through her mouth.

"She's gonna be sick," Ewan predicted in a calm voice.

"Say, Gertie," said Roy. "How do they taste?"

Gertie groaned. She'd been eating the chocolates so fast that she hadn't even tasted them.

Roy picked one up and peeled the foil away from the melted chocolate.

"You put that down!" Mary Sue squeezed her hands into fists. "That isn't for you!"

Roy ignored her and popped the chocolate in his mouth. His eyes closed. "Mmmm," he moaned. He opened his eyes. "It's got that superior smoothness." He licked his fingers. "It really has." He picked another chocolate up and passed it to June. "Try it."

People murmured.

June unwrapped the chocolate and put it in her mouth. Her eyes got big, and she brought her hand up to her lips. "Good. So good," she mumbled.

Gertie looked at the pile of chocolates on the grass. She couldn't eat another one. She would explode. Now Mary Sue would go rat on her and show everyone the chocolates.

Jean's voice broke the silence. "You can do it." Everyone stared at Jean, but she didn't even glance at them. She was watching Gertie. "Come on, Gertie," she said under her breath. "You can do it."

Gertie picked up another chocolate.

"Come on," said Jean.

Gertie unwrapped it. She put it in her mouth and chewed it up and swallowed it. She held her poor stomach. Four chocolates were left.

"She's gonna blow," Ewan warned again.

"No way," said Leo. "Come on, Gertie. You can do it."

"Stop it!" said Mary Sue. "Stop!"

"Come on, Gertie!" said June, and she started clapping.

Gertie looked up at Jean, who nodded. Gertie picked up another chocolate.

"Stop it!" Mary Sue spun around and ran toward the school, but Gertie didn't care.

Everyone was cheering. Three chocolates left. They began chanting.

"Ger-tie! Ger-tie! Ger-tie!"

Two.

It didn't matter if they were fickle. She was eating the chocolates for all of them. For June and Roy and Junior and Leo and all of them who had never been asked to take a note to the office. They were the gray crayons nobody cared about. They were the so-so students. They were the last-place losers and the skinned-kneed nobodies, and Gertie was their queen.

She stuffed the last chocolate into her mouth. Then she wadded up the last foil wrapper and threw it on the ground. *Wham!* She staggered to her feet and raised her arms in the air. "Yaaa!" she yelled.

Roy threw his own arms in the air. June and Jean were jumping up and down, hugging each other. Ewan was applauding politely. Junior was hiding his face in his hands, but he was smiling through his fingers. Then, across the playground, Gertie saw Mary Sue marching toward them. Ms. Simms was right behind her.

Gertie gulped, swallowing the final piece of evidence.

24
Everybody Messes Up

"That's what *understudy* means," said Mary Sue to anyone who would listen and lots of people who wouldn't. "It means if the actress who was *supposed* to play the part turns out to be an immature, chocolate-stealing maniac, *I* come in and save the day."

The fifth graders were filing out of the room.

"Of course," said Mary Sue, "I never should've been the understudy to start with, but now everyone knows that." She spoke in a loud voice so that Gertie heard every word. "And of course, I told my father not to expect much." She flipped her hair. "I mean, this play is perfectly ridiculous. But at least now I can help all of you look better. You're all so lucky to get to meet my father, you know, because—"

The door shut behind Ewan, catching his shirttail. Then the fabric of his shirt disappeared, and Gertie was alone with Ms. Simms while the rest of her class was rehearsing with the new and not-improved Evangelina.

This was Gertie's punishment, and it was the cruelest and unusualest punishment in the history of punishment.

She wasn't Evangelina anymore. She wasn't the Cucumber or the Ham either. She wasn't the person who helped raise the curtain. She wasn't even the person who walked up and down the aisles with a flashlight, whacking noisy people and glaring at gum-chewers.

She was nothing.

She sank lower in her seat and opened and closed her locket. *Click-snap, click-snap, click-snap.*

At the front of the room, Ms. Simms tucked a strand of hair behind her ear. As it turned out, it didn't matter whether or not Gertie had eaten the evidence, because adults didn't need evidence to punish a kid.

The principal had punished her without even hearing her side of the story. He didn't need witnesses. Even though everyone except Mary Sue swore on their lives that they hadn't seen any chocolates and that they had just found a pile of gold wrappers on the playground, which just sometimes happened, he still didn't believe them. He hadn't even *asked* Gertie if she had taken the chocolates. He just looked down his big greasy nose and bared his teeth and yelled, "Guilty!"

At least that was what it felt like. *Click-snap* went the locket. *Thump-bump* went Gertie's heels against the legs of her chair. *Click-snap.* The worst thing of all was that her mother was going to come to the play. And Gertie wouldn't have any part at all, and then her mother would know that she'd been right to leave Gertie, that she'd been right to get herself a new family, because Gertie wasn't the best fifth grader in the world. Not even close. Gertie was going to fail at her mission for the first time in her life.

"Why didn't you ask me if I'd taken the chocolates?" she blurted.

Ms. Simms glanced up from the papers she was grading. "I didn't ask," she said, "because I already knew the answer."

Gertie started to argue, but Ms. Simms cut her off.

"Gertie, you had melted chocolate from your forehead to your chin!"

"But you didn't *ask* me!" Gertie's voice scrabbled out of her throat. "I could've . . . I could've been framed. And nobody asked me *why* I would've taken them. Maybe I had a good reason."

Ms. Simms leaned back in her chair, capped her pen, and placed it on the stack of grading. "I assumed you took them so you could"—she shrugged—"*eat* them."

"Noooo," said Gertie. "It's *hard* to eat that many chocolates! No one would eat that many chocolates for fun." She took her hand off the desk and squeezed it into a fist. "It felt like my guts were about to explode, like—" Her fist burst open, fingers flinging out.

"Okay, okay," said Ms. Simms, raising a hand. "Okay. Why did you do it, then?"

"Because . . ." Gertie's voice trailed off. "Because . . ." Now that someone had asked her, she realized it was one of those things that made perfect sense to her but was very hard to explain to someone else.

Ms. Simms waited.

"Because Mrs. Warner wasn't going to give me one!" Gertie said. "She gives a chocolate to everybody, *everybody*, who takes a note to the office. But when *I* took a note to the office, she didn't give me one, and that's not fair. It's not *fair.*" Gertie tried to put as much feeling into the word as possible so that Ms. Simms would know that what Mrs. Warner had done was utterly wrong. But Ms. Simms couldn't understand. She hadn't been there. She didn't know what it felt like.

"I understand," said Ms. Simms.

"You don't under—" Gertie looked at her teacher. "What?"

"I do understand," said Ms. Simms calmly. "It doesn't seem fair to you that Mrs. Warner gives chocolates to some students but not to others." She paused. "And that *doesn't* seem nice. But they are *her* chocolates. So it's fair that she should do whatever she wants with her chocolates. Don't you think?"

Gertie didn't think so at all. "So it's fair that Mrs. Warner hates me?"

"Gertie," groaned Ms. Simms, "Mrs. Warner doesn't hate you."

"Then how come—"

"Maybe she was going to give you a chocolate if you'd waited a little longer," said Ms. Simms. "Maybe she only gives them to people who ask for them. Maybe she had something else on her mind and she forgot."

Gertie hadn't thought of that.

"All of those things are much more likely than Mrs. Warner hating you," said Ms. Simms. "Trust me."

Maybe, thought Gertie, Mrs. Warner didn't hate her. But that didn't change the fact that Ms. Simms didn't like her. "You said that you'd let me take a note to the office, but then you didn't."

Ms. Simms tilted her head and frowned. "I had you take a note to the office just yesterday."

"It was months ago," said Gertie. "Right at the beginning of the school year, you said I could take a note to the office, but then you let Mary Sue go instead. And then you said that I could take the note next time, but you didn't ask me to."

"I don't remember that," said Ms. Simms. "But I'm sure you're right. I'm sorry, Gertie."

Gertie opened her mouth and then closed it.

She wanted more than *I'm sorry.* She wanted Ms. Simms to admit that she liked Mary Sue better. She wanted Ms. Simms to say that she'd been *wrong wrong wrong* and that Gertie had been *right right right.*

"I thought the reason you never asked me to go to the office was because you didn't like me," she said.

"Of course I like you, Gertie!" Ms. Simms sounded like she meant it, but it was hard to tell. "I like you very much. I like all of my students. Whether I ask them to go to the office or not."

"Why do you choose some people more than others, then?" Gertie asked.

Ms. Simms laced her fingers together on top of her desk. "I don't put that much thought into it," she said. Half her mouth twitched up, and she leaned toward

Gertie. "Between you and me, I never choose Roy or Leo because I suspect they might get into trouble if I let them roam the halls alone."

"Everybody wants to do it." Gertie crossed her arms. "And you only let the same people do it over and over. You pick Mary Sue *all* the time. You never pick June. You never pick Junior. You never pick me." She glanced down. "Except for yesterday."

Ms. Simms was looking right at Gertie, and she had a thoughtful twist to her lips. "I guess I messed up, didn't I?"

Gertie stared. She wasn't sure she'd heard right.

"Everybody messes up," added Ms. Simms, as if she could read Gertie's mind. "Even teachers."

"But teachers aren't supposed to mess up. It's your job *not* to mess up."

"But we still mess up sometimes." Ms. Simms smiled at Gertie like she wasn't embarrassed or ashamed at all. Like being wrong and messing up was about as much cause for outrage as a case of the hiccups.

That was a fascinating idea, but Gertie couldn't mess up. She had to find some way to show Rachel Collins that she was good enough for her.

"From now on," said Ms. Simms, "I'll make sure that

everyone gets a chance to go to the office. I'll have to think up some way to keep track of whose turn it is." Her voice was thoughtful. She shook her head. "But I'll deal with that later." She looked at Gertie.

Ms. Simms was waiting for her to say something else, and that was when Gertie realized that she was running out of things to be upset about and things to explain.

Gertie folded her arms and rested her chin on them. It was possible—maybe—that Ms. Simms did like all of her students equally.

"It's kind of peaceful, isn't it?" Ms. Simms said as she picked up her grading pen again. "Having the room to ourselves."

And that she liked Gertie especially.

25
You Stupid Ham Hock!

ALL SORTS OF UNFORTUNATE ACCIDENTS MIGHT TAKE MARY Sue out of the play. For instance, she could get amnesia and forget all her lines. Or a giant zit might grow on her nose. Or she might eat so much junk food while she was training to be Evangelina that she got fat, so fat that she couldn't fit in her costume without popping all the seams. And then Gertie would be the only other one who knew the lines and everyone would beg her to be Evangelina and she would help them out because she was a nice person after all.

Aunt Rae was not as hopeful. "I think amnesia's not so common," she said as she wiped Audrey's face with a rag. "Never heard of anybody actually getting it in real life."

"But I'll be ready in case it happens. That's the point."

Aunt Rae sighed. "You know, Gertie, she—she might not come. Something might come up."

But Gertie knew she would come. She had seen it in Rachel Collins's eyes. She would be there for Gertie, which meant Gertie had to find a way to get back in the play.

All she needed was one enormous zit—green, to match Mary Sue's eyes.

She just had to keep thinking positive.

But Friday came, and Mary Sue was still zit-free.

The play was *that* night. If Gertie wasn't on the stage when Rachel Collins came, then it was all over. Gertie could never make up for that, no matter what she did.

On Friday afternoon, in the last minutes of the school day, Gertie was watching Mary Sue's hands gesture as she talked to Ella. No amnesia. No seams splitting on her shirt. Mary Sue was as perfect as ever. It was over. Unless . . . unless something happened to Mary Sue in the few hours left before the play. Unless someone stopped her . . .

"What are you going to do?"

Gertie jumped. Beside her, Jean was so focused on her copy of *Adventures in Reading, Grade 5* that Gertie almost didn't believe she had spoken.

Gertie replied in a low voice. "What are you talking about?"

"I know you've got a plan. You're going to lock Mary Sue in Stebbins's art closet, or you're going to trip her as she's going on stage. So you'll get to be in the play." Jean glanced up from her book. "So what are you going to do to her?"

Gertie didn't answer.

"You could tell me, you know." Jean frowned. "I wouldn't rat on you."

She *could* lock Mary Sue in Stebbins's closet, and then no one would be able to find her, and the play would have to go on without her, which meant that Gertie would be Evangelina again.

"I know you wouldn't rat on me," Gertie said to Jean, and she did know it.

The bell rang, and Gertie grabbed her bag and walked slowly, the crowd of yelling kids running past her. She could do it just before the play. Everyone would know that she was the best Evangelina all along. But . . .

Kidnapping Mary Sue would be like cheating, Gertie

thought. And not like cheating at cards. If she cheated on her mission, she wouldn't be able to trust herself anymore.

But what if she didn't lock Mary Sue in a closet, and she still didn't get to be Evangelina? Then she would've done her very best, and nobody would know how hard she'd worked, and she would *fail*.

By the time she got on the bus she still hadn't decided what she was going to do.

"You'll let me know before you do anything dangerous, right?" Junior pulled her out of her reverie. "Right?"

"I'm not going to . . . Why does everyone think I'm going to do something awful?" Gertie demanded. She grabbed Junior's shoulders and pulled him close until his nose was an inch from hers and she had to cross her eyes to look at him. "Do I look like an awful person?"

Junior squinted at her and tilted his head.

The Mercury was stopped in front of the school, where people were scrambling out of cars and walking into the building. Gertie unbuckled her seat belt.

"I'll find us a parking spot and then be right in," said

Aunt Rae. "Gertie, don't you think . . . I want you to know that she might . . ."

"What?" Gertie said.

"Never mind." Aunt Rae sighed.

Gertie looked from Audrey in the backseat to Aunt Rae in the front to the clock on the dash that told her she had ten minutes to do . . . something. She looked back at Aunt Rae. She'd put on purple lipstick, which was nice.

"You know what I just realized?" Aunt Rae asked suddenly.

Gertie shook her head.

"I've been mad at your mama ever since she left you," Aunt Rae said. "So mad I could spit. I never did understand how a woman could leave her own baby because she didn't feel like raising it. And I still don't understand. But I realized it doesn't matter why. I should love that woman to pieces, because she left you with me. Best thing that ever happened to me."

Gertie didn't know what to say.

"Give 'em hell, baby," Aunt Rae said then.

And Gertie knew just how to respond to that. She nodded and flung open her door and launched herself from the car. She ran across the school yard, stretching her legs as long as she could, flying past parents and

228

students who were walking toward the building. She rammed through a crowd of men waiting by the door with big cameras, which seemed strange, but she didn't have time to think about it.

Backstage, children ran around in their costumes. Ella, who was dressed as the Cucumber, was kicking a ball back and forth with someone who was wrapped in purple cellophane to look like a piece of candy. Mothers brandished glue guns and hair spray. Teachers stalked through the flurry of people, glaring at students who laughed and telling everyone to use their indoor voices *or else.*

Gertie pushed through the crowd until she found Stebbins working on June's floppy green hat, which was supposed to make her look like a Brussels sprout.

"Stebbins," said Gertie. "Stebbins, I'm here. What can I do?"

Stebbins was pulling bobby pins out of her gray bun like a magician producing endless scarves from his sleeve. She stabbed them at June's head. The green hat slipped sideways.

"Is that sanitary?" June asked. "I don't think that's sanitary. My mother says— *Oww!*"

Stebbins jabbed one last pin in and gave the hat a tug. "That should hold it."

June's eyes watered. Gertie stepped in front of Stebbins.

"Not now, Miss Foy," Stebbins snapped.

"But—"

"Tonight is the culmination of weeks of work, the realization of my vision," Stebbins said. "I suggest you stay out of my way."

Most kids would've run for their lives. Gertie planted her feet wider. "Don't you need me to do anything?"

Stebbins *tsked*. Then she said, "Find Mary Sue Spivey and have her report to me."

Gertie stood on her toes and turned, scanning the faces all around her. She didn't see any flowing yellow hair. No sparkling green eyes. No Mary Sue Spivey.

Gertie and Junior's bus driver walked into a glue-gun mother, but he didn't even notice. His lips were moving as he read a copy of the script. He was going to narrate the play. Gertie thought he was lucky to get such a big part, but he seemed nervous. He'd already eaten half a toothpick.

"I don't see her!" Gertie exclaimed, spinning back to face Stebbins. "Does that mean I get to go on?"

A bobby pin flashed dangerously close to Gertie's eye. "Find her and tell her I need to inspect her costume."

Roy bumped into Gertie as she stalked away from Stebbins. He was bumping into a lot of people, because he was wearing a giant ham hock costume made of wire and red felt.

"Stebbins, I don't want to be the Ham anymore!" said Roy.

"Tough."

"I can't look like a ham in front of Jessica Walsh." His hands waved.

"At least you're not the Potato," said Leo.

"Jessica Walsh?" Gertie stopped walking. "What about Jessica Walsh?"

"Where have you been?" asked Leo. "Jessica Walsh is *here*. In our auditorium."

Gertie sprinted to the side of the stage, where a dozen kids had squashed Junior Jr. against the wall while they pushed to peek around the curtain. Gertie elbowed Ewan out of the way.

The auditorium was crowded, but in the front row she saw the lobbyist and a man beside her who had to be Mary Sue's father, and on the other side of *him* was the one and only Jessica Walsh. She was smiling, and

232

Gertie could see her shiny white teeth all the way from behind the curtain. She looked just like her action figures, only bigger and softer. The crowd murmured and roared, and the name *Jessica Walsh* bobbed like a cork on the sea of sound.

"*I'm* in charge of the curtain," Junior was saying. "You've got to back off. You're standing on the rope."

No one was listening.

Gertie's eyes roamed around the auditorium, stopping on Aunt Rae and Audrey in the third row. Audrey was standing in her chair. Aunt Rae was squinting at her program. Beside Audrey were two empty seats they were saving. One for Gertie, just in case she didn't get to be Evangelina. One for Rachel Collins. Gertie had made Aunt Rae promise to save that seat. But it was empty. Her mother wasn't there yet.

She had *said* she was coming. Gertie stood in the huddle of her classmates and wondered. Hadn't she? Gertie thought she had. When she looked at Gertie, Gertie had been sure that she was promising she would come. But what had she said exactly?

Maybe she wasn't here because something awful had happened. For instance, maybe her mother had forgotten the time. Maybe Walter had gotten stuck in the bathtub, and she was having to chisel him out. Maybe Rachel Collins was on her way, but her car had been hijacked, and she was having to ninja the hijackers into submission.

"Jessica Walsh. She's the prettiest thing." Roy sighed. A piece of wire from his costume scratched Gertie's face. "I wish all girls were just like her."

"You're stupid," said June.

"*You're* stupid," said Roy. "That's what your problem is."

"Oh yeah? Want to know what your problem is?" June demanded.

"No," Roy said. "Not really."

Under her green hat, June's face turned red. "You stupid ham hock!"

Roy put his face an inch from June's. "Big fat broccoli."

"I'm *Brussels sprouts*!" June shoved him.

"Hey," someone yelled.

"You're on my foot!" a girl hollered.

"My curtain!" said Junior.

Gertie wriggled out of the huddle, her brain buzzing. She couldn't think about Jessica Walsh, not when she needed to focus on the mission. If Mary Sue wasn't anywhere, that meant she would get to go on!

"Have you seen Mary Sue?" she asked one of the hair-spray mothers.

The woman shook her head.

"Mary Sue?" Gertie called.

She looked in one of the first-grade classrooms they were using as a dressing room. No Mary Sue. The lobbyist and Mary Sue's father were in the audience. So Mary Sue had to be here. Only she wasn't. It was impossible. It was a miracle. It was God, rewarding Gertie for not locking Mary Sue in the closet! She was going to be Evangelina!

This was the answer to everything.

Gertie popped her head in the bathroom. "Hello?" she called. She waited, counting, *One-Mississippi, two-Mississippi.* No answer. Mary Sue wasn't here either. Yes!

But as Gertie was leaving, the restroom door swinging closed behind her, she heard a loud *honk.*

Maybe she had imagined the honk. Maybe it was nothing. She started to turn back to the staging area, where she would find Stebbins and tell her that Mary Sue wasn't there, and she, Gertie Reece Foy, would have to be their Evangelina.

But Gertie couldn't stand maybes. She turned around and pushed the door open. She stepped into the girls' room.

Jean was standing at one of the stalls, passing someone a handful of toilet paper. Gertie went further in and
looked around Jean.

Mary Sue was sitting on a toilet, crying. And she wasn't
crying her beautiful diamond tears. Gertie had *known*
those diamond tears were fake. Mary Sue's face was red,
and her eyes were almost swollen shut.

26

More Bath Tissue

IT WAS BY NO MEANS A ZIT OF UNUSUAL SIZE, BUT MARY
Sue's tearstained face was still a spectacularly swollen
mess.

"G-go away!" Mary Sue dabbed her eyes with a wad
of toilet paper.

Jean shrugged one shoulder at Gertie, which had an
exciting effect because she was wearing a sweatshirt
covered in empty soda cans. They were taped on every
inch of her shirt so that she looked like she was wearing
homemade battle armor.

"What's wrong?" Gertie asked.

"Nothing's wrong!" Mary Sue scrubbed at her face.

Gertie looked over her shoulder at the bathroom door,
which had just swung shut. She could still hear the

rumble of the auditorium crowd. She turned back to Mary Sue. "Are you hurt or something?"

"What do you care?" Mary Sue sniffed. "You've tried to ruin things for me ever since I moved here. You've hated me from the very beginning. You probably hope I *die*." She hiccupped.

Once upon a time—maybe two minutes ago—Gertie *had* thought that she wanted Mary Sue to cry her eyes out in a germy old bathroom stall. But now that she was here, watching Mary Sue twist bits of toilet paper, she didn't want this after all.

"I thought you'd be happy," Gertie said. "I mean, Jessica Walsh is here, you know?"

Jean shook her head.

Mary Sue made a sound that was something between a sob and a scream, and Gertie stepped backward and fell into a sink. "Of course I know *she's* here. M-my father b-b-brought her here from Los Angeles."

"He came all the way from California," Gertie whispered because it seemed like such an unbelievable thing, that your father would get on an airplane and fly across the country, just to see Stebbins's mortifying nutrition play.

"Well, I don't know why he bothered." Mary Sue

sounded like she had a bad cold. "Jessica Walsh is better at being his daughter than I am. Did you know she came to my birthday party and signed autographs during the cake and gelato, and—and everyone was so busy *worshipping* her that all the gelato melted?"

"Umm," said Jean.

Gertie didn't know what to say either. "That's bad, huh?"

Mary Sue ignored them. "And even if I make good g-g-grades it doesn't matter because *Jessica Walsh* makes good grades, and she doesn't even go to real school." Mary Sue's fingers tore the toilet paper into confetti that littered the floor. "And if I'm good in the play, nobody's going to care because Jessica Walsh was an actress f-first, and"—Mary Sue wiped her nose with the back of her hand—"after the play she'll tell everyone what I did wrong, and she'll say that *she* could've done it better."

Jessica Walsh sounded like someone who needed to have dirt rubbed in her face. Gertie looked at Jean, thinking it was Jean's turn to say something encouraging.

"It could be worse," said Jean.

"What?" Mary Sue looked up.

"I mean," said Jean, "this seems bad, but you know . . . it could get worse."

Gertie knew she was trying, but Jean was no good at encouraging.

"It *is* worse," Mary Sue said. "Can you get me more bath tissue?"

What kind of person said *bath tissue*? A Mary Sue Spivey kind of person, Gertie guessed.

Jean and her soda cans clanked into an empty stall and ripped off at least five feet of toilet paper.

"My mother says we're not going back to California." Mary Sue wiped her face. "She says her work is *soooo* important here. She says we're going to live here, in this horrible town, if you can even call it a town. P-permanently."

"Oh my Lord."

"I know," Mary Sue agreed. She looked at her feet. "I told her I'd go live with my father. But . . . but he said it was better that I stay here. Because they're—they're getting a divorce." She hiccupped. "How can they do this to me?" she wailed.

Gertie didn't know what to say.

"Sooo . . ." Jean looked from Gertie to Mary Sue. "What are we doing now?"

"The show must go on. I guess you'll have to do it," said Mary Sue, looking at Gertie. "That's p-perfect. I'll just sit on this toilet while you steal my part."

"I wasn't going to *steal* your part!" Gertie exclaimed, her voice bouncing off the bathroom walls. "And *I* was Evangelina first!"

Mary Sue waved a hand. "Everyone likes you best. Everyone thinks you're so wonderful. Even though you're a horrible person, and you're ignorant about oil and the environment and—"

"I'm not a horrible person!" Gertie said. Mary Sue thought everyone liked *her* best? All this time, she had been trying to beat Mary Sue, and Mary Sue had been trying to beat her so that she could show up Jessica Walsh.

Honestly. Mary Sue should've just rubbed dirt in Jessica Walsh's face.

At that moment, Mary Sue's words finally sank in. "Wait, you want me to be Evangelina?" Gertie asked.

"Of course I don't *want* you to be Evangelina. But I can't do it, and no one else knows the lines."

Gertie did still know the lines. Backwards, forwards, and sideways. She could do it. "The play must go on. Like you said."

Mary Sue sniffed. Jean shrugged and clanked.

Gertie couldn't believe that everything was going to work out after all. This was why it paid to never give up. She should be getting herself ready for her moment when her mother would realize she was a star. Gertie imagined how Rachel would look, smiling up at Gertie from the audience. Her eyes would crinkle, and she would realize that Gertie had become the most amazing fifth grader in the world.

Mary Sue had just said that everyone loved Gertie best, that everyone thought she was wonderful. It wasn't true. People were fickle. But her mother would like Evangelina. Everyone liked Evangelina. That was the point of her.

Gertie knew that her father would say she shouldn't have to change so that someone would like her.

Gertie clutched her locket. But he was on the rig. She was the one who would have to make the decision, because he was far, far away. Distance was strange though. Mary Sue's father had flown across a whole country to be here. But Gertie had had to beg her mother just to drive across town. Maybe that was why Rachel Collins hadn't gone any further than Jones Street when she left the first time. Maybe three miles could be further than three thousand.

Gertie worked her thumbnail into the locket's groove and looked inside at the tiny picture of a baby in a woman's hands. She had worked harder than she'd ever worked before, and she'd wanted to make Rachel Collins know she was important, and now she was realizing that maybe Rachel Collins wasn't worth it.

"You can do it," she said. She snapped the locket shut and let it go.

Mary Sue looked up.

Gertie took a deep breath. She knew that Rachel Collins would be proud of her if she were Evangelina. But Gertie wanted her mother to be proud of her just like she was. "You can do it," she said. "You should be Evangelina. I mean, your daddy came to see you. And Jessica Walsh will be horrible if you don't do it."

"She would," said Mary Sue. "She really would. You have no idea how awful she is."

"We could guess," said Jean.

"Are you sure?" asked Mary Sue.

Gertie nodded, and Mary Sue's eyebrows rose in shock, like she'd never seen Gertie before. Even though she had a lot on her mind, when she saw Mary Sue's expression, a tiny part of Gertie couldn't help but feel like she was a sweet-angel-fairy-godmother person. She could almost feel herself twinkle.

Mary Sue stood up. She looked in the mirror, and her lip trembled. "I can't," she whimpered. "I look hideous."

"You don't look that bad," said Jean. "I mean, it could be worse."

"Here." Gertie grabbed Mary Sue's bag off the floor and peered inside. Jean raised her eyebrows at the brushes and pots and tubes.

"We've got to make you look presentable." Gertie grabbed a pouf. She swished it through some powder and slapped it on Mary Sue's damp face, which left chunks of powder that kind of looked like corn flakes.

Mary Sue coughed. "Stop! Stop it!"

Jean bent over at the hips, her soda-can sweatshirt getting in the way, and picked up Evangelina's dress.

"What are you doing? You'll wrinkle it!" Mary Sue snatched it from her.

Gertie grabbed a hairbrush. She was going to fix Mary Sue's hair all nice and maybe give it just one good yank. She was that kind of fairy-godmother person.

27
I'm Fatty and Delicious

THE AUDITORIUM WAS DARK. THE AIR WAS HUMID WITH THE breath of proud parents and grandparents and bored brothers and sisters and tired teachers and out-of-town relatives and old Uncle Martys. Gertie squeezed past knees and stumbled over shoes as she scurried along the third row.

The curtain rose and polite applause rippled through the crowd. Gertie shuffled past Aunt Rae. Audrey scooted sideways into one of the seats they'd been saving to make space. Gertie collapsed into the chair between them with a *thunk*.

"Shh," someone shushed behind them.

"Is everything okay?" Aunt Rae whispered.

"Yes," Gertie whispered back.

"Shh."

Mary Sue walked onto the stage. Her face was flour white and crumbly from all the makeup, and her eyes were still puffy from crying. She looked around at the audience for a long time. Too long. Gertie began to think she had forgotten the lines. Then Mary Sue's eyes stopped on Jessica Walsh, and she stood straighter and lifted her chin.

"I'm Evangelina," she announced in a loud, nasal voice, "and I have a sweet tooth." She smiled and pointed at one of her teeth.

The whole room sighed. They began to enjoy the play, and soon half of Gertie's classmates skipped out in their candy and soda and junk food costumes. The Ham trailed onto the stage, arms hanging by his sides.

"I'm fatty and delicious," Roy said in a flat voice, "but not very nutritious."

When Evangelina sat up after her serious illness, rubbing her eyes, beaming at her new healthy friends, and thanking them for saving her and destroying all the unhealthy food, the audience cheered. Mr. Spivey actually stood up and applauded, which was nice. He had puny forearms, though. Not everyone's father could be big and strong, Gertie thought.

Aunt Rae reached out and grabbed her knee. Gertie looked at the wrinkled fingers and put her own hand over Aunt Rae's. On her other side, Audrey twisted in her seat to see what they were doing. Then she crawled over Gertie, her knees digging into Gertie's guts, her elbow swiping Gertie's nose.

"Oof," groaned Gertie.

Lying across Gertie's lap, Audrey put her hand on Aunt Rae's knee.

"Shh," shushed the person behind them again.

"Like church mice," Audrey hissed at Gertie.

Gertie watched Junior, heaving at the ropes to control the curtain, and Mary Sue, lifting her chin as she faced Jessica Walsh, and Roy, red-faced in his ham-hock costume, and Jean, serious in her clanky soda-can sweatshirt. The entire cast was marching onto the stage for a final bow.

The seat beside Audrey's was still empty. Gertie tried not to look at it. For the first time in her life, she had failed at her mission. She had done everything she could think of, and she hadn't given up, and she'd been nice to the seat-stealer . . . And she'd still failed.

Ms. Simms had made it seem like messing up was a piece of cake. But it wasn't. It was a stomachache. Gertie let out a long sigh. Maybe Ms. Simms had had more practice.

Everyone on stage bowed, and the audience began to get to their feet and clap. Aunt Rae stood, too.

Most kids in Gertie's situation wouldn't ever go on a mission again. Most kids would do what everyone told them and stop coming up with their own ideas. Most kids would cross their arms and refuse to clap for a stuffy-nosed Evangelina who said things like *bath tissue*.

But Gertie was not, had never been, and would never be like most kids. She leaped up and climbed onto her chair, bringing her hands together hard. Because in the end, as always, Gertie was exactly like herself.

EPILOGUE
Glory, Glory, Glory

THE BULLFROG CROUCHED BENEATH THE ZAPPER-2000. HE was waiting for a bug to fly into the big blue beacon and have the everlasting daylights zapped out of it.

Fried flies for me, the bullfrog sang. *Baked buggies. Cooked little critters. Glory, glory, glory.*

The yellow bus—Mr. Monster Frog-Squisher—squealed to a stop in front of the house. The frog-grabber girl ran across the yard, sandals kicking up dust.

"Give 'em hell, baby!" boomed a voice.

The girl leaped into the bus's belly. She'd be back, he knew. She always came back. But he was safe for now.

He gazed up into the blue beacon. Zombie Frog was home, which was perfect.